Susanna Moodie

The Monctons
Volume 2

outlook

Susanna Moodie

The Monctons
Volume 2

1st Edition | ISBN: 978-3-75244-027-0

Place of Publication: Frankfurt am Main, Germany

Year of Publication: 2020

Outlook Verlag GmbH, Germany.

Reproduction of the original.

THE MONCTONS:

A NOVEL.

BY
SUSANNA MOODIE.
IN TWO VOLUMES.

VOL II.

CHAPTER I.

"The next day, my friend bade us adieu. Had he expressed the least wish to that effect, I would have accompanied him to the South—but he did not, and we parted, never to meet again. He died abroad, and Charlotte became the inheritor of his large fortune. Her grief for the loss of her brother affected her health and spirits to such an alarming degree, that instant change of air and scene was recommended by her physician, and she left London to spend some months with her aunt on the Continent. I would have gladly made one in their party, but this she forbade me to do in the most positive terms.

"I fancied that her manner to me had grown cold and distant during the separation which had intervened between her brother's death and the severe illness that followed the announcement of that melancholy event. These fears were confirmed by a long and very prudential letter from her aunt, entreating me, as a mutual friend, not to follow them to Italy, as it might be attended by unpleasant results to Miss Laurie, who was still very young—too young, in her estimation, to acknowledge publicly an accepted lover; that as no actual engagement existed between us, she thought it most advisable for both parties only to regard each other in the light of friends, until the expiration of the time which would make Miss Laurie the mistress of her hand and fortune. It was impossible to mistake the purport of this letter, which I felt certain must have been sanctioned by her niece. Then, and not until then was I fully aware of all that I had lost by the death of my poor friend.

"Charlotte had repented of her affection for the low-born Philip Mornington. She was a great heiress now, and a match for the first nobleman in the kingdom. I crushed the letter beneath my feet, and felt within my breast the extinction of hope.

"I suspected that Robert Moncton and his son were at the bottom of this unexpected movement; nor was I mistaken. It was strange, that among the whole range of my acquaintance, I had never been introduced to this rascal and his son, or met him accidentally at any place of public resort. They effectually worked my ruin, but it was in the dark.

"The loss of Charlotte made me reckless of the future. I plunged headlong into all sorts of dissipation: wine, women, the turf, the gaming-table, by turns intoxicated my brain, and engrossed my time and thoughts, until repeated losses to an alarming amount, made me restless and miserable, without in the least checking the growing evil. I had forfeited self-respect, and with it the moral courage to resist temptation.

"I was goaded on in my career of guilt by a young man of fascinating person and manners, but of depraved habits and broken fortunes. From the first night that I was introduced to William Howard, he expressed for me the deepest respect and friendship, and haunted me subsequently like my shadow. He flattered my vanity by the most sedulous attentions, echoed my sentiments, hung upon my words, copied my style of dress, and imitated my manners.

"These arts might have failed in producing the desired effect, had he not wound himself into my confidence, by appearing to sympathize in my mental sufferings. He talked of Charlotte, and endeavoured to soothe my irritated feelings, by expressing the most sanguine hopes of my ultimate success; and, to dissipate the melancholy that preyed upon my health and spirits, he led me by degrees to mix with the reckless and profligate, and to find pleasure in the society of individuals whom I could not respect, and from whose proximity a few months before I should have shrunk with disgust and aversion.

"A young fellow just beyond his minority is easily led astray, particularly, when he has wealth at his command, and no settled employment or profession to engage his time and thoughts, and worse still, with no religious principles to guide him in his perilous voyage across the treacherous ocean of life.

"Alas! Geoffrey; I chose for my pilot one who had not only ruined himself, but caused the shipwreck of others, superior in prudence and intelligence; to the man who now trusted to his advice and believed him a friend.

"When I look back to that disastrous period of my life, my soul shrinks within itself, and I lament my madness with unceasing bitterness. All that I have since suffered, appears but a just retribution for those three years of vice and folly. Little did I then suspect, that my quondam friend was an infamous sharper, bribed by the still more infamous Robert Moncton to lure me to destruction.

"In spite of her aunt's prohibition, I had continued to write to Miss Laurie; at first, frequently, seldom many days elapsing between letter and letter, but to my surprise and indignation, not one of my communications had been answered, although breathing the most ardent attachment, and dictated by a passion as sincere as ever animated a human breast. What could be the cause of this cruel neglect? I called repeatedly at Mrs. ———'s house in town, but was constantly told by the old housekeeper, who received me very coldly, that Miss Laurie and her aunt were still on the continent.

"As long as this miserable state of uncertainty continued, I clung to hope, and maintained the character of a man of honour and a gentleman. But the insidious tempter was ever at hand, to exaggerate my distress, and to weaken my good resolutions. Howard laughed at my constancy to a false mistress, and by degrees, led me to consider myself as a very ill-used man, and Miss Laurie as a heartless coquette.

"Two years had elapsed since the death of Cornelius; and I was just ready to accompany a party of gay young fellows to Newmarket, when I was told accidentally, that Miss Laurie, the great heiress, had arrived in town, and the young men were laughing and speculating upon the chance of winning her and her fortune.

"'They say she's a beauty!' cried one.

"'Beauty won't pay debts,' said another. 'I can't afford to marry for love.'

"'A plain girl with her property is sure to be handsome. Beauty and gold are too much to fall to the share of one person. I dare say, she's only passable.'

"'Sour grapes, Hunter,' said Howard. 'You know that you are such a —— ugly fellow, that no woman, with or without a fortune would take you for better or worse.'

"'*Better* is out of the question, Howard, and he can't be well worse,' said the first speaker. 'But I should like to know if Miss Laurie is really the beauty they say she is. Money is a thing to possess—to enjoy—to get rid of. But beauty is a divinity. I may covet the one—I adore the other.'

"'You may do both then, at a humble distance, George. But here's Philip Mornington, can satisfy all your queries—he knows, and used to feel an interest in the young lady.'

"To hear her name in such company, was to me profanation. I made some ungracious reply to what I considered an impertinent observation of Howard's, and feigning some improbable excuse for absenting myself from the party, I turned my horse's head and rode back to my lodgings, in spite of several large bets that I had pending upon a favorite horse.

"Charlotte was in London, and I could not rest until I had learned my fate from her own lips. I hastened to her aunt's residence; and, contrary to my expectations, on sending up my card, I was instantly admitted to her presence.

"She was alone in the drawing-room. The slight girl of seventeen was now a beautiful and graceful woman; intelligence beaming from her eyes, and the bloom of health upon her cheek. As I approached the table at which she was seated, she rose to meet me, and the colour receded so fast from her face that I feared she would faint, and instead of addressing me with her usual frankness, she turned away her head and burst into tears.

"You may imagine my distress: I endeavoured to take her hand, but she drew proudly back.

"'Is this Charlotte?'

"'Rather let me ask—is this Philip Mornington, my brother's friend?' she spoke with a degree of severity which astonished me—'the man for whom I once entertained the deepest respect and affection.'

"'Which implies that you do so no longer?'

"'You have rightly guessed.'

"'And may I ask Miss Laurie why she has seen fit to change the opinion she once entertained?'

"'Mr. Mornington,' said she, firmly, repressing the emotion which convulsed her lips and glistened in her eyes, 'I have long wished to see you, to hear from your own lips an explanation of your extraordinary conduct, and though this meeting must be our last, I could not part with you for ever, until I had convinced you that the separation was effected by yourself.'

"'It will be difficult to prove that,' said I, 'if you really sanctioned your aunt's letter, and were privy to its contents.'

"'It was written at my request,' she replied, with provoking coldness. 'Mr. Moncton's suspicions were aroused, and your following us to the continent would have confirmed them, and rendered us both miserable. But my motives for requesting a temporary separation, were fully discussed in my letter which accompanied the one written by my aunt. To this reasonable request you returned no answer, nor, in fact, to several subsequent letters which were written during our absence abroad.'

"I trembled with agitation while she was speaking, and I fear that she misinterpreted my emotion.

"'Good Heavens!' I exclaimed at last, 'how grossly have I deceived myself into the belief that you never wrote to me—that you cast me from you without one word of pity or remorse. I never got a line from you, Charlotte. Your aunt's cruel letter came only too soon, and was answered too promptly; and to the many I have written to you since, you did not deign a reply.'

"'They never reached us, Mr. Mornington; and it is strange that these letters (which to me were, at least, matters of no small importance) should be the only ones among the numbers addressed to us by other friends, which miscarried.'

"I was stung by the incredulous air with which she spoke: it was so unlike my own simple, frank-hearted Charlotte.

"'Miss Laurie, you doubt my word?'

"'A career of vice and folly, Mr. Mornington, has made me doubt your *character*. While I could place confidence in the *one*, I never suspected deceit in the other.'

"'Your silence, Charlotte, drove me to desperation, and involved me in the dissipation to which you allude.'

"'A man of integrity could not so easily be warped from the path of duty:' she said this proudly. 'I can no longer love one whom I have ceased to respect, whose conduct, for the last two years, has made me regret that we ever met.'

"'You are too severe, Miss Laurie,' and I felt the blood rush to my face. 'You should take into account all I have suffered for your sake.'

"'You found a strange method of alleviating those sufferings, Philip.' This was said sadly, but with extreme bitterness. 'Had you loved or cherished me in your memory, you never could have pursued a course of conduct so diametrically opposite to my wishes.'

"This was a home-thrust. I felt like a guilty and condemned creature, debased in my own eyes, and humbled before the woman I adored.

"I felt that it was useless to endeavour to defend myself against her just accusations; yet, I could not part with her, without one struggle more for forgiveness, and while I acknowledged and bitterly lamented my past errors, I pleaded for mercy with the most passionate eloquence. I promised to abjure all my idle companions and vicious habits, and devote the rest of my life entirely to her.

"She listened to me with tearful earnestness, but remained firm to her purpose, that we were to part there for ever, and only remember each other as strangers.

"Her obstinacy rendered me desperate. I forgot the provocation I had given her by my wicked and reckless course. I reproached her as the cause of all my crimes. Accused her of fickleness and cruelty, and called Heaven to witness, how little I merited her displeasure.

"Her gentle feminine brow was overcast; her countenance was dark and stern.

"'These are awful charges, Mr. Mornington. Permit me to ask you a few questions, in my turn, and answer them briefly and without evasion.'

"I gazed in silent astonishment upon her kindling face.

"'Are you in the habit of frequenting the gaming-table? Yes, or no.'

"My eyes involuntarily shrunk from hers.

"'The race-course?'

"'I must confess to both these charges,' I stammered out. 'But'——

"'For such conduct there can be no excuse. It is not amid such scenes that I would look for the man I love.'

"'Cease, Charlotte, in mercy cease, if you do not mean to drive me mad. Some enemy has poisoned your mind against me. Left to yourself, you could not condemn me in this cold, pitiless manner.'

"'Your own lips have condemned you, Philip.' She stopped, passed her hand across her brow, as if in sudden pain, and sighed deeply.

"'When will these reproaches end, Charlotte? Of what else do you accuse me?'

"'Is what I have said, false or true?' she cried, turning suddenly towards me, and grasping my arm. 'If false, clear yourself. If true, what more can I have to do with you?'

"'Alas!' I cried, 'it is but too true!'

"'And can you expect, Mr. Mornington, that any virtuous, well-educated woman could place her happiness in the keeping of one who has shown such little self-government; who chooses for his associates men of loose morals and bad character. Your constant companion and bosom friend is a notorious gambler, a man whose society is scouted by all honourable men. I pity you, Philip; weep for you; pray for you; and God only knows the agony which this hour has cost me; but we must meet as lovers and friends no more.'

"She glided from the room, and I stood for some minutes stupidly staring after her, with the horrible consciousness of having exchanged a pearl of great price, for the base coin in which pleasure pays her deluded followers, and only felt the inestimable value of the treasure I had lost, when it was no longer in my power to recover it.

"I returned to the company I had quitted. I betted and lost; plunged madly on; staked my whole property on a desperate chance, and returned from the races, forsaken by my gay companions, a heart-broken and ruined man!

"It was night when I reached London. Not wishing to encounter any of my late associates, I entered a coffee-house seldom frequented by men of their class, and called for a bottle of wine.

"The place was ill-lighted and solitary. I threw myself into a far corner of my box, and, for the first time (for I never was a drinker) tried to drown care in the intoxicating bowl.

"The wine, instead of soothing, only increased the fever of my spirit, and I began to review with bitterness the insanity of my conduct for the last few months. With a brain on fire with the wine, I continued eagerly to swallow, and a heart as dull and cold as ice from recent mortification and disappointment, I sank with my head upon the table into a sort of waking trance, conscious of surrounding objects, but unable to rouse myself from the stupor which held every faculty in its leaden grasp.

"Two men entered the box. I heard one say to the other, in a voice which seemed familiar.

"'This place is occupied, we had better go to another.'

"'The fellow's drunk,' returned his companion, and may be considered as *non compos*. He has lost all knowledge of himself, and therefore can take no notice of us.'

"Feeling little interest in anything beyond my own misery, I gave no signs of life or motion, beyond pressing my burning brow more tightly against my folded hands, which rested on the table.

"'So, Mornington's career is ended at last, and he is a ruined man,' said the elder of the twain.

"'Yes, I have settled his business for you; and as my success has been great, I expect my reward should be proportionately so.'

"'I am ready to fulfil my promise, but expect nothing more. You have been well paid by your dupe. He has realized the old proverb—Light come, light go. I thought he would have given you more trouble. Yours, Howard, has been an easy victory.'

"'Hang the foolish fellow!' cried my quondam friend; 'I feel some qualms of conscience about him; he was so warm-hearted and generous—so unsuspicious, that I feel as if I had been guilty of a moral murder. And what, Mr. Moncton, must be your feelings: your hatred to the poor young man is almost gratuitous, when it appears that you are personally unknown to each other.'

"'He is the son of my worst enemy, and I will pursue him to death.'

"'He will spare you the trouble, if I read my man rightly. He will not submit to this sudden change of fortune with stoical indifference, but will finish a career of folly with an act of madness.'

"'Commit suicide?'

"'Ay, put a pistol to his head. He is an infidel, and will not be scared from his purpose by any fear of an hereafter.'

"'Bring me that piece of news to-morrow, Howard, and it will be something to stake at hazard before night.'

"He left the box; I rose to prevent him, but the opportunity of revenge was lost. The younger scoundrel remained behind to settle with the waiter; as he turned round I confronted and stared him full in the face. He pretended not to know I who was.

"'Fellow, let me pass!'

"'Never! until you have received the just reward of your treachery. You are a mean, contemptible wretch: the base hireling of a baser villain. I will prosecute you both for entering into a conspiracy against me.'

"'You had better let it alone,' said he, in a hoarse whisper. 'You are a disappointed and desperate man. No sensible person will listen to complaints made by a drunken, broken-down spendthrift and gambler.'

"'Liar!' I cried, losing all self-control, 'when did you ever see me drunk, or knew me guilty of one dishonourable act?'

"'You were always too great a fool, Mornington, to take care of yourself, and you are not able, at this moment, to stand steady. Be that, however, as it may, I never retract my words; if you require satisfaction, you know where to find me.'

"'I will neither meet nor treat you as a gentleman. You are beneath contempt.'

"'The son of a drunken huntsman has a greater claim to gentility,' sneered the sharper, bursting into an insulting laugh. 'Your mother may, perhaps, have given you an indirect claim to a higher descent.'

"This taunt stung me to madness, and sobered me in a moment. I flung myself headlong upon him. I was young and strong—the attack unexpected, he fell heavily to the ground. In my fury I spat upon him, and trampled him beneath my feet. Death, I felt was too honourable a punishment for such a contemptible villain. I would not have killed him though certain that no punishment would follow the act.

"The people of the house interfered. I was taken into custody and kept in durance vile until the following morning; but as no one appeared to make any charge against me, I was released, with a severe reprimand from the police magistrate, and suffered to return home.

"Home! I had now no home: about one hundred pounds was all that remained to me of my fine property when my debts, falsely termed debts of honour, were paid, my lodgings settled for, and my servant discharged.

"My disgrace had not yet reached the home of my childhood. A state of mental suffering brought on a low fever. I was seized with an indescribable longing, an aching of the heart to end my days in my native village.

"Pride in vain combated this feeling. It resisted all the arguments of reason and common sense. Nature triumphed—and a few days saw me once more under the shadow of the great oak which canopied our lowly dwelling."

CHAPTER II.
ALICE.

"As I approached the cottage door, my attention was arrested by a low, mournful voice, singing in sad and subdued tones, a ditty which seemed the spontaneous outpouring of a wounded spirit. The words were several times repeated, and I noted them down as I leant upon the trunk of the old tree. Out of sight, but within a few feet of the songstress, whose face was hidden from me by the thick foliage of the glorious old tree, in whose broad-spreading branches, I had played and frolicked when a boy.

"'THE SONG.

I once was happy, blithe and gay,
    No maiden's heart was half so light;
I cannot sing, for well a-day!
    My morn of bliss is quenched in night.
I cannot weep—my brain is dry,
    Deep woe usurps the voice of mirth
The sunshine of youth's cloudless sky
    Has faded from this goodly earth.
My soul is wrapped in midnight gloom,
    And all that charmed my heart before,
Droops earthward to the silent tomb,
    Where darkness dwells forevermore.'

"The voice ceased. I stepped from my hiding-place. Alice rose from the bench beside the door; the work on which she was employed fell from her hand, and she stood before me wild and wan—the faded spectre of past happiness and beauty.

"'Good heavens! Alice, Can this be you?'

"'I may return the compliment,' she said, with a ghastly smile. 'Can this be Philip? Misery has not been partial, or your brow wears its mark in vain.'

"'Unhappy sister of an unhappy brother!' I cried, folding her passive form to my heart, 'I need not ask why you are altered thus.'

"The fire which had been burning in my brain for some weeks, yielded to softer emotions. My head sunk upon her shoulder, and I wept long and bitterly.

"Alice regarded me with a curious and mournful glance, but shed no tears.

"'Alice! That villain has deceived you?'

"She shook her head.

"'It is useless to deny facts so apparent. Do you love him still?'

"She sighed deeply. 'Yes, Philip. But he has ceased to love me.'

"'Deserted you?'

"Her lip quivered. She was silent.

"'The villain! his life shall answer for the wrong he has done you!'

"The blood rushed to her pale, wasted cheeks, her eyes flashed upon me with unnatural brilliancy, and grasping my arm, she fiercely and vehemently replied—

"'Utter that threat but once again, and we become enemies for life. If he has injured me and made me the wreck you see—it is not in the way you think. To destroy him would drive me to despair. It would force me to commit an act of desperation. I will suffer no one to interfere between me and the man I love. I am strong enough to take my own part—to avenge myself, if need be. I can bear my own grief in silence, and therefore beg that you will spare your sympathy for those who weep and pule over misfortune. I would rather be reproached than pitied for sorrows that I draw upon myself.'

"She sat down trembling with excitement, and tried to resume her former occupation. Presently the needle dropped from her hand, and she looked wistfully up in my face:—

"'Philip, what brought you here?'

"'An unwelcome visitor, I fear.'

"'Perhaps so. People always come at the worst times, and when they are least wanted.'

"'Do you include your brother in that sweeping common-place term—has he become to you as one of the people? Ah, Alice.'

"'We have been no more to each other for the last three years, Philip. Your absence and long silence made me forget that I had a brother. Few could suppose it, from the little interest you ever expressed for me.'

"'I did not think of you, or love you the less.'

"'Mere words. Love cannot brook long separation from the object beloved. It withers beneath neglect, and without personal intercourse droops and dies. While you were happy and prosperous you never came near us; and I repeat again—what brings you now?'

"'I have been unfortunate, Alice; the dupe of villains who have robbed me of my property, while my own folly has deprived me of self-respect and peace of mind. Ill and heart-sick, I could not resist the strong desire to return to my native place to die.'

"'There is no peace here, Philip,' said she, in a low soft voice. 'I too, would fain lie down on the lap of mother earth and forget my misery. But we are too young—too wretched to die. Death comes to the good and happy, and cuts down the strong man like the flower of the field; but flies the wretch who courts it, and grins in ghastly mockery on the couch of woe. Take my advice, Philip Mornington, lose no time in leaving this place. Here, danger besets you on every side.'

"'Why, Alice, do you think I fear the puny arm of Theophilus Moncton—the base betrayer of innocence.'

"'Why Theophilus. Spare your reproaches, Philip; we shall quarrel seriously if you mention that name with disrespect to me—I cannot, and will not bear it. It was not him I meant. You have offended our grandmother by your long absence, Dinah loves you not. It is her anger I would warn you to shun.'

"'And do you think I am such a coward, as to tremble and fly from the malice of a peevish old granny?'

"'You laugh at my warning, Philip. You may repent rashness when too late. The fang of the serpent is not deadened by age, and the rancour in the human heart seldom diminishes, with years. Dinah never loved you, and absence has not increased the strength of her affection.'

"'I am not come to solicit charity, Alice. I have still enough to pay the old woman handsomely for board and lodging until my health returns, or death terminates my sufferings. If Dinah takes me—a fact I do not doubt—she loves money. Where is she now?'

"'In the village, I expect her in every minute.'

"'And Miss Moncton?' I said, hesitating, and lowering my voice. 'How is she?'

"'I don't know,' returned Alice, carelessly, 'the Hall is no longer open to me.'

"'That tells its own tale,' said I sorrowfully.

"'The tale may be false, in spite of probability,' returned she fiercely. 'No one should dare openly condemn another without sufficient evidence.'

"'They need not go far for that,' said I.

"'That is your opinion.'

"'On most conclusive evidence.'

"'How charitable.'

"'How true, Alice.'

"'False as the world. As you, as every one is to the unfortunate,' she cried, with indignation in her eyes and scorn upon her lip, 'but here is Dinah—Dinah, whom you consider unfeeling and cruel. She knows me, and loves me better than you do. She does not join with a parcel of conventional hypocrites to condemn me.'

"As she ceased speaking, Dinah entered with a basket on her arm. After the first surprise at my unexpected and unwelcome appearance was over, she accosted me with more amenity of look and manner than I ever before knew her to assume.

"'How are you, Philip? you look ill. Suppose you have got into some trouble, or we should not be honoured by a visit?'

"'You are right, in part, grandmother. I have been sick for some days, and have come home for change of air and good nursing.'

"I put a handful of gold in her lap. 'You see I am willing and able to pay for the trouble I give. When this is gone, you can have more.'

"'Money is always welcome—more welcome often than those that bring it. All things considered, however, I am glad to see you. When relatives are too long separated, they become strangers to each other. Alice and I had concluded that you only regarded us as such. The sight of you will renew the old tie of kindred, and make you one of us again. Quick, Alice, get your brother some supper; he must be hungry after his long journey.'

"'I am in no need; Alice, do not trouble yourself; I feel too ill to eat; I will go to bed if you please. All I want at present is *rest.*'

"Dinah, who was passing the gold from one hand to the other, and gazing upon it with infinite satisfaction, suddenly looked up and repeated the last word after me, with peculiar emphasis.

"'*Rest!* Who rests in this world? Even sleep is not rest; the body sleeps, but the soul toils on, on, on, for ever. There is no such thing as rest. If I thought so, I would put an end to my existence to-morrow—I would; and meet death as a liberator from the vexatious turmoils of life.'

"There was something in these words which filled my mind with an indescribable horror—a perfect dread of endless duration. I had always looked upon the grave as a place of rest—a haven of peace from the cares of life. That old raven, with her dismal croaking, had banished the pleasing illusion, and made me nervously sensitive to the terrors of a living, conscious eternity. Whilst undressing to go to bed, I was seized with violent shivering fits, and before morning was delirious, and in a high fever.

"I had never suffered from severe illness before; I had often been afflicted in mind, but not in body. I now had to endure the horrors of both combined. For the first fortnight I was too ill to think. I was in the condition of the unfortunate patriarch, who in the morning exclaimed, 'Would God it were night!' and when night came, reversed the feverish hope.

"There were moments, however, during the burning hours of these sleepless nights, when the crimes of the past, and the uncertainty of the future, rushed before me in terrible distinctness; when I tried to pray and could not, and sought comfort from the Word of God, and found every line a condemnation. Oh, those dreadful days and nights, when I lay a hopeless, self-condemned expectant of misery, shuddering on the awful brink of eternity, shrieking to the Almighty Father for peace, and finding none; seeking for rest with strong cries and tears, and being repaid with ten-fold agony. May I never again suffer in flesh and spirit what I then endured!

"The poor lost girl who watched my bed, beheld the fierce tossings of pain, the agonies of remorse, the icy apathy. She could neither direct nor assist my mind in its struggles to obtain one faint glimmer of light through the dense gloom caused by infidelity and sin.

"Death—natural death—the mere extinction of animal life, I did not dread. Had the conflict ended with annihilation, I might have welcomed it with joy. But death unaccompanied by total extinction was horrible. To be deprived of moral life—to find the soul for ever separated from God, all its high and noble faculties destroyed, while all that was infamous and debasing remained to form a hell of memory, an eternity of despair, was a conviction so dreadful, so appalling to my mind, that my reason for a time bowed before it, and for some days I was conscious of nothing else.

"This fiery trial yielded at last. I became more tractable, and could think more calmly upon the awful subject ever uppermost in my mind. I felt a strong desire to pray, to acknowledge my guilt to Almighty God, and sue for pardon, and restoration to peace and happiness. I could not express my repentance in words, I could only sigh and weep, but He who looks upon the naked human heart, knew that my contrition was sincere, and accepted the unformed petition.

"As the hart panteth for the water brooks, so did my thirsty soul pant for the refreshing waters of life. In feeble tones I implored Alice to read to me from the New Testament. My eyes were so much affected by the fever, that I could scarcely distinguish the objects round me.

"The request was distasteful, and she evaded it for many days—at last, replied testily.

"'There is not such a book in the house—never was; and you know that quite well.'

"'You can borrow one from the schoolmaster in the village.'

"'I will do no such thing. A pretty story truly, to go the rounds of Moncton. That the Morningtons were such godless people they had no Bible in the house, and had to borrow one. They say that Dinah is a witch, and that would confirm it.'

"'Send the boy that cuts sticks in the wood. Let him ask it as if for his mother. I know Mr. Ludd will lend it for a good purpose; and tell the boy I will give him half a sovereign for his pains.'

"'Nonsense! Why that would buy the book.'

"'Oh, do buy it, Alice, my good angel; for the love of God! send and buy it. You will find my purse in my coat-pocket. It will be the best money that was ever laid out by me.'

"'You had better be still and go to sleep, Philip; you are too ill to bear the fatigue of reading yet.'

"This was dreadfully tantalizing, but I was forced to submit. The next morning she brought me a cup of tea. I looked wistfully in her face.

"'Dear Alice, you could give me something that would do me more good than this.'

"'Some broth, perhaps; sick people always fancy everything that is not at hand.'

"'That book.'

"'Are you thinking about that still?'

"'I long for the bread of life.'

"'Do you want to turn Methodist?'

"'I wish to become a Christian.'

"'Are you not one already?'

"'Oh, no, no, Alice! All my life long I have denied the word of God and the power of salvation; and now, I would give the whole world, if I possessed it, to obtain the true riches. Do, dear sister, grant my earnest request, and may the God of all mercy bring you to a knowledge of the truth.'

"'I hate cant,' said Alice, discontentedly, 'but I will see what I can do for you.'

"She took some money from my purse and left the room.

"Hours passed away. I listened for her returning footsteps until I fell asleep. It was night when I again unclosed my eyes. Alice was sitting by the little table reading. Oh, blessed sight. The Bible lay open before her.

"'I dreamt it,' I cried joyfully. 'I dreamt that you got it, and God has brought it to pass. Oh, dear Alice you have made me so happy.'

"'What shall I read?

"I was puzzled; so much had I become a stranger to the sacred volume, that though it had formed a portion of my school and college studies, the little interest then felt in its contents, had made me almost a stranger to them.

"'Read the Gospel of St. John.'

"'A chapter you mean.'

"'As much as you can. Until you are tired.'

"She began at the opening chapter of that sublime gospel, in which we have so much of the mind of Jesus, though less of his wondrous parables and miracles; but matter which is higher, more mysterious, spiritual and satisfying to the soul. Nor could I suffer her to lay aside the book until it was concluded.

"How eagerly I drank in every word, and long after every eye was closed in sleep I continued in meditation and prayer. A thousand times I repeated to myself, 'And ye shall know the truth, and the truth shall set you free,' What a glorious emancipation from the chains of sin and death! Oh, how I longed for a knowledge of that truth, and the answer came:—'O Lord thy word is truth;' and the problem in my soul was satisfied, and with a solemn thanksgiving I devoted myself to the service of God. A calm and holy peace came down upon my soul, and that night I enjoyed the first refreshing sleep I had known for many weeks.

"In the morning I was much better, but still too weak to leave my bed.

"I spent most of the day in reading the Bible. Alice had relaxed much of her attention and I only saw her during the brief periods when she administered medicine, or brought me broth or gruel.

"I felt hurt at her coldness; but it was something more than mere coldness. Her manner had become sullen and disagreeable. She answered me abruptly and in monosyllables, and appeared rather sorry than glad, that I was in a fair way of recovering.

"I often heard her and Dinah hold confused whispering conversations, in the outer room into which mine opened, the cottage being entirely on the ground floor, and one evening I thought I recognized the deep tones of a man's voice. I tried to catch a part of their discourse, but the sounds were too low and guarded to make anything out. A short time after I heard the sound of horses' hoofs upon the gravel walk which led past the cottage into the park. I sat up in the bed which was opposite the window, which commanded a view of the road, and perceived, to my dismay, that the stranger was no other than Robert Moncton, who was riding towards the village.

"A dread of something—I scarcely knew what—took possession of my mind, and remembering my weak, helpless state, and how completely I was in the power of Dinah North, I gave myself up to vague apprehensions of approaching evil.

"Ashamed of my weakness, I took the sacred volume from under my pillow, and soon regained my self-possession. I felt that I was in the hands of God, and that all things regarding me would be ordered for the right. Oh, what a blessing is this trust in the care of an overruling Providence! how it relieves one from brooding over the torturing fears of what may accrue on the morrow, verifying the divine proverb: 'Sufficient unto the day is the evil thereof!'

"A thick, dark, rainy night had closed in, when my chamber door opened, and Alice glided in. She held in her hand a small tray, on which was a large tumbler of mulled wine and some dry toast. I had not tasted food since noon, and I felt both faint and hungry. A strange, ghastly expression flitted over my sister's face, which was unusually pale, as she sat down on the side of the bed.

"'You have been a long time away,' said I, with the peevish fretfulness of an invalid. 'If you were ill and incapable of helping yourself, Alice, I would not neglect you, and leave you for hours in this way. I might have died during your absence.'

"'No fear of that, Philip. You are growing cross, which is always a good sign. I would have come sooner, but had so many things to attend to, that it was impossible. Dinah is too old to work, and all the household work falls on me. But, how are you?'

"'Better, but very hungry.'

"'I don't doubt it. It is time you took something. I have got a little treat for you—some fine mulled sherry—it will do you good and strengthen you.'

"'I don't care for it,' said I, with an air of disgust. 'I am very thirsty. Give me a cup of tea.'

"'We got tea hours ago, when you were asleep, and there is not a drop of hot water in the kettle. The wine is more nourishing. The doctor recommended it. Do taste it, and see how good it is!'

"'I tried to comply with her request. A shudder came over me as I put the tumbler to my lips. 'It's of no use,' I said, putting it back on to the tray. 'I cannot drink it.'

"'If you love me, Philip, try. Drink a little, if you can, I made it on purpose to please you.'

"She bent her large bright eyes on me with an anxious, dubious expression —a strange, wild look, such as I never saw her face wear before.

"I looked at her in return, with a curious, searching gaze. I did not exactly suspect her of any evil intention towards me, but her manner was mysterious, and excited surprise.

"She changed colour, and turned away.

"A sudden thought darted through my brain. Robert Moncton had been there. He coveted my death, for what reason I could not fathom. I only knew the fact. What if that draught were poison!—and suspicion, once aroused, whispered it is poison.

"I rose slowly in the bed, and grasped her firmly by the wrist.

"'Alice! we will drink of that glass together. You look faint and pale. The contents will set you all right. Take half and I will drink the rest.'

"'I never drink wine.'

"'You dare not drink *that* wine,' said I.

"'If I liked it, what should hinder me?'

"'You could not like it, Alice. It is *poison*!'

"A faint cry burst from her lips.

"'God of heaven! who told you that?'

"'Flesh and blood did not reveal it to me. Alice, Alice, how could I imagine such a thing of you?'

"'How, indeed!' murmured the wretched girl, weeping passionately. '*She* persuaded me to bring it to you. *He* mixed the wine. I—I had nothing else to do with it.'

"'Yet to you, as a willing instrument of evil, they entrusted the most important part of their hellish mission.'

"She flung herself on her knees beside the bed, and raising her clasped hands and streaming eyes to Heaven implored God to forgive her for the crime she had premeditated against my life, binding herself in an awful curse, not only to devise means to save my life, but to remove me from the cottage.

"'As to you, Philip, I dare not ask you to forgive me: I only implore you not to curse me.'

"'I should entertain a very poor opinion of myself, if I should refuse to do the one, or attempt such an act of wickedness as is involved in the other. But, Alice, do not think that I can excuse the commission of such a dreadful crime as murder—and upon whom? A brother who loved you tenderly—who, to his own knowledge, never injured you in word, thought or deed.'

"'Philip, you are not my brother, or the deed had never been attempted.'

"'Not your brother! Who am I then?'

"'I cannot—dare not tell you. At least not now. Escape from this dreadful place, and some future time may reveal it.'

"'You talk of escape as a thing practicable and easy. I am so weak I can scarcely stand, much less walk ten paces from the house. How can I get away unknown to Dinah?'

"'Listen to me—I will tell you.' She rose from her knees, and gliding to the door which led to the outer room, she gently unclosed it, and leaning forward looked cautiously into the outer space. Satisfied that it was vacant, she returned stealthily to my bed-side.

"'I must make Dinah believe that you have drank this wine. In less than two hours you will, in her estimation, be dead. Not a creature knows of your return. For our own sakes, we have kept your being here a profound secret. Robert Moncton, however, was duly informed by Dinah of your visit. He came this morning to the house, and they concocted this scheme between them. She is now absent looking for a convenient spot for a grave for your body when dead. She talked of the dark shrubbery. That spot is seldom visited by any one, because the neighbours fancy that it is haunted. You know how afraid we were of going near those dark, shadowy yews when we were children. Margaret used to call it the valley of the shadow of death.'

"'And it was there,' said I, with a shudder, 'that you meant to bury me?'

"'There—I have promised to drag your body to the spot in a sack, and help Dinah to make your grave. But hist! I thought I heard a step. We have no time to waste in idle words.'

"'She cannot bury me, you know, without my consent, before I am dead,' said I, with a faint smile. 'Nor can I imagine how you will be able to deceive her. She will certainly discover the difference between an empty sack and a full one.'

"'I have hit on a plan, which, if well managed, will lull her suspicions to sleep. You know the broken statue of Apollo, that lies at the entrance of the Lodge? It is about your size. It once belonged to the Hall gardens, and Sir Alexander gave it to me for a plaything years ago. I did not care for such a huge doll, and it has lain there ever since. I will convey this to your chamber, and dress it in your night-clothes. The sack will cover the mutilated limbs, and by the dim, uncertain light of the dark lantern, she will never discover the cheat.'

"'But if she should insist on inspecting the body?'

"'I will prevent it. In the meanwhile you must be prepared to leave the house when I come to fetch the body.'

"I felt very sick, and buried my face in the pillows.

"'I do not care to go; let me stay here and die.'

"'You must live for my sake,' cried the unhappy girl, clasping my cold hand to her heart, and covering it with kisses. 'If you fail me now, we are both lost. Dinah would never forgive me for betraying her and Moncton. Do you doubt that what I have told you is true?'

"'Not in the least, Alice; but I am so weak and ill—so forsaken and unhappy, that I no longer care for the life you offer.'

"'It was the gift of God. You must not throw it away. He may have work on the earth which he requires you to do.'

"These words saved me. I no longer hesitated to take the chance she offered me, though I entertained small hopes of its success. Yet if the hand of Providence was stretched out to rescue me from destruction, it was only right for me to yield to its guidance with obedient gratitude and praise.

"Alice was about to leave the room: she once more returned to my side.

"'Say that you forgive me, Philip.'

"I folded her in my thin wasted arms, and imprinted a kiss on her rigid brow.

"'From my very heart!'

"'God bless you! Philip. I will love and cherish your memory to my dying hour.'

"The house-door opened suddenly; she tore herself from my embrace. 'Dinah is coming—lie quite still—moan often, as if in pain, and leave me to manage the rest.'

"She left the chamber, and the door purposely ajar, that I might be guided in my conduct by what passed between them.

"'Did he drink it?' whispered the dreadful woman.

"'He did.'

"'And how does it agree with his stomach?' she laughed—her low, horrid laugh.

"'As might be expected—he feels *rather* qualmish.'

"'Ha, ha,!' cried the old fiend, rubbing her withered long hands together, 'you came Delilah over him. Our pretty Samson is caught at last. Let me see—how long will it be before the poison takes effect—about two hours—when did he take it?'

"'About an hour ago. He is almost insensible. Don't you hear him groan. The struggle will soon be over.'

"'And then my bonny bird will have no rival to wealth and power. What your mother, by her obstinate folly, lost, your wit and prudence, my beauty, will regain.'

"This speech of Dinah's was to me perfectly inexplicable. I heard Alice sigh deeply, but she did not reply.

"The old woman left the cottage but quickly returned.

"'I want the spade.'

"'You will find it in the out-house; the mattock is there, too; you will need it to break the hard ground.'

"'No, no; my arm is strong yet—stronger than you think, for a woman of my years. The heavy rain has moistened the earth. The spade will do the job; we need not make a deep grave. No one will ever look for him there.'

"'The place was always haunted, and it will be doubly so now.'

"'Pshaw! who believes in ghosts. The dead are dead—lost—gone for ever; grass springs from them, and their juices go to fatten worms and nourish the weeds of the earth. Light me the lantern and I will defy all the ghosts and demons in the world; and hark you, Alice, the moment he is dead put the body in a sack, and call me to help to drag it to the grave. I shall have it ready in no time.'

"'Monster!' I muttered to myself, 'the pit you are preparing for me, ere long, may open beneath your own feet.'

"I heard the old woman close the front door after her, and presently Alice re-entered my chamber.

"'Well, thank God she is gone on her unholy task. Now, Philip! now—lose no time—rise, dress yourself, and get off as fast as you can!'

"I endeavoured to obey, but exhausted by long sickness I fell back fainting upon the bed.

"'Stay,' said Alice, 'you are weak for the want of nourishment. I will get you food and drink.'

"She brought me a glass of port wine, and some sandwiches. I drank the wine eagerly, but I could not touch the food. The wine gave me a fictitious strength. After making several efforts I was able to rise and dress, the excitement of the moment and the hope of escape acting as powerful stimulants. I secured all that remained of my small fund of money, tied up a change of linen in a pocket-handkerchief, kissed the pale girl who stood cold and tearless at my side, and committing myself to the care of God, stole out into the dark night.

"I breathed again the fresh air, and my former vigour of mind returned. I felt like one just freed from prison, after having had sentence of death pronounced against him, I was once more free; I had miraculously escaped from death and danger, and silently and fervently I offered up a grateful prayer to the Heavenly Father, to whom I was indebted for such a signal act of mercy.

"You will think it strange, Geoffrey—the whim of a madman—but I felt an insatiable curiosity to witness the interment of my supposed body, to see how Alice would carry out the last act of the tragic drama.

"The wish was no sooner formed, than I prepared to carry it into execution.

"The yew shrubbery lay at the north end of the cottage, and was divided from the road, by a clipped holly hedge. A large yew tree grew out of the centre of this hedge, which had been clipped to represent a watch tower. Open spaces having been left for loop-holes. Through these square green apertures, I had often, when a boy, made war upon the blackbirds and sparrows, unseen by my tiny game.

"By creeping close to the hedge, and looking through one of these loop-holes, I could observe all that was passing within the shrubbery, without being observed by Dinah or Alice. Cautiously stealing along, for the night was intensely dark, and guiding my steps by the thick hedge, which resembled a massy green wall, I reached the angle where it turned off into the park. In this corner stood the green tower I was seeking, and climbing softly the gate which led into the spacious domain of the Monctons, I stepped upon a stone block used by the domestics for mounting horses, and thus raised several feet from the ground, I could distinctly observe, through the opening in the tree, all that was passing below.

"A faint light directly beneath me, gleamed up in the dense drizzly darkness, and shone on the hideous features of that abhorred old woman, who was leaning over a shallow grave she had just scooped out of the wet dank soil. Her arms rested on the top of the spade, and she scowled down into the pit that yawned at her feet, with a smile of derision on her thin sarcastic lips.

"'It's deep enough to hide him from the light of day. There's neither a shroud nor coffin to take up the room, and he is worn to a skeleton by his long sickness. Yes; there let him rest till the judgment-day! the worm for his mate and the cold clay for his pillow; I wish the same bed held all his accursed race. And his pale-faced, dainty mother—where is she? Does her spirit hover near, to welcome her darling to the land of dreams?'

"A light step sounded on the narrow path which led from the shrubbery to the cottage, accompanied by a dull lumbering sound.

"Dinah raised the lantern from the side of the grave, and held it up into the dark night.

"'Alice?'

"'Dinah!'

"'Is he dead?'

"'Yes. Here, lend a hand. The body is dreadfully heavy. I am almost killed with dragging it hither.'

"'You did not bring it alone!'

"'Who could I ask to help me? and I was so afraid of discovery, I dared not leave it to come for you.'

"The old woman put down the light, and went to help her granddaughter.

"'Let us roll the body into the grave, mother.'

"'Not yet—I must look at him.'

"'He makes a dreadful corpse.'

"'Death is no flatterer, child. Hold up the light.'

"'No, no!—You must not—you shall not triumph over him now. Let the dead rest, I dare not look upon that blue cold face, those staring eyes again.'

"'Who wants you, foolish child? I wish to satisfy myself that my enemy is dead.'

"A scuffle ensued, in which the light was extinguished, and the supposed body rolled heavily over into the grave.

"'Oh, mother, mother! the light is out, and we're alone with the corpse in this dreadful darkness.'

"'Nonsense! how timid you are! Go back to the house, and re-light the candle.'

"'I dare not go alone.'

"'Then let me go?'

"'And leave me with him? Oh, not for worlds. Mother, mother! I hear him moving in the grave. He is going to rise and drag me down into it. Look—look! I see his eyes glaring in the dark hole. There, mother—there!'

"'Curse you for a weak fool! You make even my flesh creep.'

"'Cover it up—cover it up!' cried Alice, pushing with her hands and feet some of the loose earth into the grave. 'That ghastly face will rise and condemn us at the Last Day. It will haunt me as long as I live. Oh, 'tis terrible, terrible, to feel the stain of blood on your soul, and to know that all the waters of the great ocean could never wash it out.'

"'I will go home with you, Alice, and return and close the grave myself,' said Dinah, in a determined tone. 'If you stay here much longer, you will make me as great a coward as yourself.'

"I heard the sound of their retreating steps, and leaving my place of concealment, slowly pursued my way to the next village. Entering a small tavern, I asked for a supper and a bed. The innkeeper and his wife were both known to me, but I was so much altered by sickness that they did not recognize me. After taking a cup of tea, I retired to rest, and was so overcome by mental and bodily fatigue, that I slept soundly until noon the next day, when I breakfasted, and took a seat in the mail coach for London.

"During my journey I calmly pondered over my situation, and formed a plan for the future, future, which I lost no time in putting into practice.

"From what had fallen from the lips of Alice, I was convinced that some mystery was connected with my birth, and the only means which I could devise to fathom it, was to gain more insight into the character and private history of Robert Moncton.

"At times the thought would present itself to my mind that this man might be my father. My mother was a strange creature—a woman whose moral principles could not have ranked very high. I scarcely knew, from my own experience, whether she possessed any—at all events I determined to get a place in his office, if possible, and wait patiently until something should turn up, which might satisfy my doubts, and expose the tissue of villainy which an untoward destiny had woven around me. While at college, I had gained an extensive knowledge in the jurisprudence of my country—in which I took great delight, and which I had intended to follow as a profession; when, unfortunately, the death of Mr. Mornington rendered me an independent man. At school I had learned to write all sorts of hands, and could engross with great beauty and accuracy.

"As a man, I was personally unknown to Robert Moncton, whom I never beheld but once, and for a few minutes only, when a boy, and time and sickness had so altered me, that it was not very likely that he would recognize me again.

"Two years previous to the time of which I am now speaking, I had saved the eldest son of Mr. Moncton's head clerk from drowning, at the risk of my own life. Mr. Bassett was overwhelming in his expressions of gratitude, and as to his poor little wife, she never mentioned the circumstance with dry eyes. The boy, who was about ten years of age, was a very noble, handsome little fellow, and I often walked to their humble lodgings to see him and his good parents, who always received me with the most lively demonstrations of joy.

"To these good people I determined to apply for advice and assistance. Fortunately my application was made in a lucky moment. Mr. Bassett was about to leave your uncle's office, and he strongly recommended me to his old master, as a person well known to him; of excellent character, and who was every way competent to fill his place.

"I was accepted. You know the rest."

"Our friendship, dear Geoffrey," said Harrison, concluding the narrative of his life, "rendered my situation far from irksome, while it enabled me to earn a respectable living. At present, I have learned little which can throw any additional light upon my sad history. Alice Mornington still lives, and is about to become a mother. Theophilus, the dastardly author of her wrongs, is playing the lover to the beautiful Catherine Lee, who is a ward of his father's.

"From the conversation which passed between Dinah North and Mr. Moncton in your chamber, I suspect that my poor Alice is less guilty than she appears. Dinah has some deeper motive than merely obliging Robert Moncton, in wishing to make you illegitimate. I feel confident that this story has been recently got up, and is an infamous falsehood. If true, you would have heard of it before, and I advise you to leave no stone unturned to frustrate their wicked conspiracy."

"But what can I do?" said I. "I have neither money nor friends; and my uncle will take precious good care that no one in this city shall give me employment."

"Go to Sir Alexander. He expressed an interest in your situation. Tell him the story of your wrongs, and, depend upon it, he will not turn a deaf ear to your complaint. I know that he hates both father and son, and will befriend you to oppose and thwart them."

My heart instantly caught at this proposal.

"I will go!" I cried. "But I want the means."

"I can supply you with the necessary funds," said George Harrison—for I must still call him by his old name. "And my offer is not wholly disinterested. Perhaps, Geoffrey, you may be the means of reconciling your friend to his old benefactor. But this must be done cautiously. Dinah North must not know that I am alive. Her ignorance of this fact places this wicked woman in our power, and may hereafter force her to reveal what we want to know."

I promised implicit obedience to these injunctions, and thanked him warmly for his confidence and advice. His story had made a deep impression on my mind. I longed to serve him. Indeed, I had become very warmly attached to him; regarding him in the light of a beloved brother.

In a fortnight, I was able to walk abroad, and was quite impatient to undertake my Yorkshire journey. Harrison was engaged as a writer in the office of a respectable solicitor in Lincoln's Inn Fields, and we promised to correspond regularly with each other during my absence. He generously divided with me the little money he possessed, and bidding God bless and prosper my journey, bade me farewell. I mounted the York stage, and for the first time in my life, bade adieu to London and its environs.

CHAPTER III.
MY VISIT TO MONCTON PARK.

It was a fine, warm, balmy evening in May—green delicious May. With what delight I gazed abroad upon the face of Nature. Every scene was new to me, and awakened feelings of curiosity and pleasure.

Just out of a sick-bed, and after having been confined for weeks in a dusky, badly-ventilated and meanly-furnished garret, my heart actually bounded with rapture, and, I drank in health and hope from the fresh breeze which swept the hair from my pale brow and hollow cheeks.

Ah, glorious Nature! beautiful, purest of all that is pure and holy! Thou visible perfection of the invisible God. I was young then, and now am old, but never did I find a genuine love of thee, dwelling in the heart of a deceitful, wicked man. To love thee, we must adore the God who made thee; and however sin may defile what originally He pronounced good, when we return with child-like simplicity to thy breast, we find the happiness and peace which a loving parent can alone bestow.

Nothing remarkable occurred during my journey. The coach in due time deposited me at the gates of the Lodge, in which my poor friend Harrison had first seen the light. An involuntary shudder ran through me, when I recognized old Dinah North, standing within the porch of the cottage.

She instantly knew me, and drew back with a malignant scowl.

Directing the coachman to leave my portmanteau at the village inn until called for, I turned up the broad avenue of oaks that led to the Hall.

The evening was calm and lovely. The nightingale was pouring his first love-song to the silent dewy groves. The perfume of the primrose and violet made every swelling knoll redolent of sweets. I paused often, during my walk, to admire the beauty of a scene so new to me. Those noble hills and vales; that bright-sweeping river; those towering woods, just bursting into verdure, and that princely mansion, rising proudly into the blue air—all would be mine, could I but vindicate my mother's honour, and prove to the world that I was the offspring of lawful wedlock.

I felt no doubt myself upon the subject. Truth may be obscured for a while, but cannot long remain hid. The innate consciousness of my mother's moral rectitude never for a moment left my mind—a proud conviction of her innocence, which, I was certain, time would make clear.

Full of these reflections, I approached the Hall. It was an old-fashioned building, which had been created during the wars of York and Lancaster, now venerable with the elemental war of ages, and might in its day have stood the shock of battle and siege. It was a fine old place, and associated as it was with the history of the past sent a thrill of almost superstitious awe through my heart.

For upwards of three hundred years it had been the birth-place of my family. Here they had lived and flourished as Lords of the soil; here, too, most of them had died, and been gathered into one common burial-place, in the vault of the picturesque gothic church, which stood embosomed in trees not far from the old feudal mansion.

And I, the rightful heir of the demesne, with a soul as large,—with heart and hand equal to do and dare, all that they in their day and generation had accomplished—approached the old home, poor and friendless, with a stigma upon the good name, which legally I might never be able to efface.

But, courage, Geoffrey Moncton! He who first added the appendage of Sir to that name, rode among the victors at the battle of Cressy, and the war-shout of one of his descendants rang out defiantly on the bloody field of Agincourt! Why need you despair? England wants soldiers yet, and if you fail in establishing your claims to that name and its proud memories, win one, as others have done before you, at the cannon's mouth.

I sent up my card, which gained me instant admittance. I was shown into the library, which Harrison had so often described. A noble old room panelled to the ceiling, with carved oak now almost black with age. Here I found the Baronet engaged with his daughter in a game at chess. He rose to meet me with evident marks of pleasure, and introduced me to Miss Moncton, as a young cousin, in whom he felt much interested, and one with whom he hoped to see her better acquainted.

With a soft blush, and a smile of inexpressible sweetness, the little fairy, for she was almost as diminutive in stature, bade me welcome.

Her face, though very pleasing, was neither striking nor beautiful. It was, however, exquisitely feminine, and beaming with intelligence, dignity and truth. Her large, dark, soul-lighted eyes were singularly beautiful. Her complexion, too fair and pale for health; the rich ruby-coloured full lips and dazzling teeth, forming a painful contrast with the pure white cheeks, shaded by a dark cloud of raven tresses, which, parting on either side of her lofty brow, flowed in rich curls down her snowy neck, and over her marble shoulders to her waist.

Her figure in miniature comprised all that was graceful and lovely in woman; and her frank, unsophisticated manners rendered her, in spite of a faulty mouth, very attractive.

After exchanging a few sentences, Miss Moncton withdrew, and I lost no time in explaining to her father the cause of my visit; the manner in which I had been treated by my uncle, my recent illness, and the utter friendlessness of my position. "You told me, sir, to come to you at any crisis of difficulty, for advice and assistance. I have done so, and shall feel most grateful for your counsels in the present emergency. I am willing and able to work for my bread; I only want an opening to be made in order to get my own living."

"Your profession, Geoffrey; why not stick to that?"

"Most gladly would I do so, had not Robert Moncton put the finishing stroke to his tyranny, by tearing my indentures, and by this malicious act destroyed the labour of seven years."

"The scoundrel! the mean, cowardly scoundrel!" cried Sir Alexander, striking the table with such violence with his clenched hand, that kings, queens, knights, bishops and commoners made a general movement to the other side of the chess-board. "Never mind, Geoffrey, my boy, give me your hand—I will be your friend. I will restore you to your rights, if it costs me the last shilling in my purse—ay, or the last drop in my veins. Let the future for a short time take care of itself. Make this your home; look upon me as your father, and we shall yet live to see this villain reap the reward of his evil deeds."

"Generous, noble man!" I cried, while tears of joy and gratitude rolled down my cheeks: "how can I ever hope to repay you for such disinterested goodness?"

"By never alluding to the subject, Geoffrey. Give me back the love your father once felt for me, and I shall be more than repaid. Besides, my lad, I am neither so good nor so disinterested as you give me credit for. I detest, despise that uncle of yours, and I know the best way to annoy him is to befriend you, and get you safe out of his villainous clutches. This is hardly doing as I would be done by, but I can't help it. No one blames another for taking a fly out of a spider's web, when the poor devil is shrieking for help, although he be the spider's lawful prey; but who does not applaud a man for rescuing his fellow man from the grasp of a scoundrel! By-the-by, Geoffrey," added he, "have you dined?"

"At the last inn we stopped at on the road."

"The Hart; a place not very famous for good cheer. Their beef is generally as hard as their deer's horns. Let me order up refreshments."

"By no means. You forget, Sir Alexander, that of late I have not been much used to good living. The friend on whose charity I have been boarding is a poor fellow like myself."

"Well, we must have our chat over a glass of old wine."

He rang the bell. The wine was soon placed upon the table, and most excellent wine it proved. I was weak from my long confinement to a sick chamber, and tired with my long journey; I never enjoyed a glass of wine so much in my life.

"What do you think of Moncton, Geoffrey?"

"It is a glorious old place."

"Wish it were yours—don't you? Confess the truth, now."

"Some fifty years hence," said I, laughing.

"You would then be too old to enjoy it, Geoffrey; but wait patiently God's good time, and it may be yours yet. There was a period in my life," and he sighed a long, deep, regretful sigh, "when I hoped that a son of mine would be master here, but as that cannot be, I am doomed to leave no male heir to my name and title, I know no one whom I would rather see in the old place than my cousin Edward's son."

"Your attachment to my father must have been great, when, after so many years, you extend it to his son."

"Yes, Geoffrey, I loved that wild, mad-cap father of yours better than I ever loved any man; but I suffered one rash action to separate hearts formed by nature to understand and appreciate each other. You are not acquainted with this portion of the family history. Pass the bottle this way, and I will enlighten your ignorance."

"When your grandfather, in the plenitude of his worldly wisdom (for he had a deal of the fox in his character), left the guardianship of his sons to his aged father, it was out of no respect for the old gentleman, whom had cast him off rather unceremoniously, when his plebeian tastes led him to prefer being a rich citizen, rather than a poor gentleman; but he found, that though he amassed riches, he had lost caste, and he hoped by this act to restore his sons, for whom he had acquired wealth, to their proper position in society.

"My grandfather, Sir Robert, grumbled a good deal at being troubled with the guardianship of the lads in his old age. But when he saw those youthful scions of his old house, he was so struck with their beauty and talents, that from that hour they held an equal place in his affections with myself, the only child of his eldest son, and heir to his estates.

"I was an extravagant, reckless young fellow of eighteen, when my cousins first came to live at Moncton; and I hailed their advent with delight. Edward, I told you before, had been an old chum of mine at school; and when Robert was placed in a lawyer's office, he accompanied me to college to finish my education. He was intended to fill his father's place in the mercantile world, but he had little talent or inclination for such a life. All his tastes were decidedly aristocratic, and I fear that my expensive and dissipated habits operated unfavourably on his open, generous, social disposition.

"With a thousand good qualities, and possessing excellent qualities, Edward Moncton was easily led astray by the bad example of others. He was a fine musician, had an admirable voice, a brilliant wit, and great fluency of speech, which can scarcely be called advantageous gifts, to those who don't know how to make a proper use of them. He was the life of the society in which we moved, courted and admired wherever he went, and a jolly time we had of it, I can tell you, in those classical abodes of learning, and frequently of sin.

"Edward gave me his whole heart, and I loved him with the most entire affection. But, though I saw that my example acted most perniciously on his easy disposition, I wanted the moral courage to give up a course of gaiety, in order to save him from ruin.

"Poor Edward!—I would give worlds to recall the past. But the bad seed was sown, and in time we reaped the bitter fruits.

"With all my faults, I was never a gambler; women, wine, and extravagant living, were my chief derelictions from the paths of rectitude. But even while yielding to these temptations, I was neither an habitual drunkard nor a profligate, though I frequented haunts, where both characters were constantly found, and ranked many such men among my chosen friends and associates. My moral guilt, was perhaps as great as theirs; for it is vain for a man to boast of his not being intemperate, because nature has furnished him with nerves which enable him to drink, in defiance to reason, quantities which would deprive the larger portion of men of their senses.

"Your father thought, boy like (for he was full three years my junior), to prove his title to manhood by following closely in my steps, and too soon felt the evil effects of such a leader. He wasted his health in debauchery, and wine maddened him. The gaming-table held out its allurements, he wanted fortitude to resist its temptation, and was the loser to a considerable amount. He kept this a secret from me. He was a minor, and he feared that it might reach my grandfather's ears, and that Sir Robert would stop the supplies, until his debts were paid. I heard of it through a mutual friend, and very consistently imagined the crime far greater than any that I had committed.

"The night before we left college, I followed him to his favourite rendezvous, held in the rooms of a certain young nobleman, unknown to the authorities, where students who were known to belong to wealthy parents, met to play hazard and écarté, and lose more money at a sitting, than could be replaced by the economy of years.

"I was not one of Lord ——'s clique, and I sent my card to Edward by a friend, requesting to speak to him on a matter of importance. After some delay, he came out to me. He was not pleased at being disturbed, and was much flushed with wine.

"'What do you want, Alick?' said he, in no very gentle tones.

"'I want you to come and help me prepare for our journey to-morrow.'

"'There will be plenty of time for that, by-and-by. I am engaged, and don't choose to be dictated to like a school-boy.'

"'You are mad,' said I, taking hold of his arm, 'to go there at all. Those fellows will cheat you out of every penny you have.'

"'That's my own look-out. I tell you once for all, Alick, I don't choose you to ride rough-shod over me, because you fancy yourself superior. I will do as I please. I have lost a deal of money to-night, and I mean to play on until I win it back.'

"You will only lose more. You are not in a fit state to deal with sharpers. You are so tipsy now, you can hardly stand.'

"As I said this, I put my arm around him to lead him away, when he, maddened I suppose by drink and his recent losses, burst from me, and turning sharp round, struck me a violent blow on the face. 'Let that satisfy you, whether I am drunk or sober,' he exclaimed, and with a bitter laugh, returned to the party he had quitted.

"Geoffrey, I felt that blow in my heart. The disgrace was little in comparison to the consciousness that it came from his hand—the hand of the friend I loved. I could have returned the injury with ten-fold interest; but I did nothing of the sort. I stood looking after him with dim eyes and a swelling heart, repeating to myself—

"'Is it possible that Edward struck me?'

"That blow, however, achieved a great moral reformation. It led me to think—to examine my past life, and to renounce for ever those follies, which I now felt were debasing to both soul and body, and unworthy the pursuit of any rational creature.

"The world expected me, as a gentleman, to ask satisfaction of Edward for the insult I had received.

"I set the, world and its false laws at defiance.

"I returned to my lodgings and wrote him a brief note, telling him that I forgave him, and gently remonstrating with him on the violence of his conduct.

"Instead of answering, or apologizing for what he had done, he listened to the advice of a pack of senseless idiots, who denounced me as a coward, and lauded his rash act to the skies.

"To seek a reconciliation, would be to lose his independence, they said, and prove to the world that he had been in the wrong. I, on my part, was too proud to solicit his friendship, and left London before the effort of mutual friends had effected a change in his feelings.

"Perhaps, as the injurer, he never forgave me for being the originator of the quarrel: be that as it may, we never met again. My grandfather died shortly after. I formed an unfortunate attachment to a person far beneath me in rank, and but for the horror of entailing upon myself her worthless mother, would certainly have made her my wife. To avoid falling into this snare, I went abroad for several years, and ultimately married a virtuous and lovely woman, and became a happy husband and father, and I hope a better man."

The Baronet ceased speaking for a few minutes, then said with a half smile.

"Geoffrey, men are sad fools. After losing that angel, I came very near marrying my old flame, who was a widow at the time, and as handsome as ever. She died most opportunely, I am now convinced, for my comfort and respectability, and I gave up all idea of taking a second wife."

This account tallied exactly with Harrison's story, which had given me a key to the Baronet's history. I inquired, rather anxiously, if he and my father remained unreconciled up to the period of his death.

"'I wrote to him frequently, Geoffrey,' he replied, 'when time had healed the wound he inflicted on my heart, but he never condescended to reply to any of my communications. I have since thought that he *did* write, and that his brother Robert, who was always jealous of our friendship, destroyed the letters. I assure you, that this unnatural estrangement formed one of the saddest events in my life; and for the love I still bear his memory, I will never desert his orphan son.'"

I thanked the worthy Baronet again and again, for the generous treatment I had received from him, and we parted at a late hour, mutually pleased with each other.

CHAPTER IV.

A SAD EVENT.

A few weeks' residence found me quite at home at the Hall. My new-found relatives treated me with the affectionate familiarity which exists between old and long-tried friends. I ceased to feel myself the despised *poor relation*; a creature rarely loved and always in the way, expected to be the recipient of all the kicks and cuffs of the family to whom his ill-fortune has made him an attaché, and to return the base coin with smiles and flattering speeches.

Of all lots in this hard world, the hardest to bear must be that of a domestic drudge; war, war to the knife is better than such humiliating servitude. I could neither fawn nor cringe, and the Baronet, who was a high-spirited man himself, loved me for my independence.

The summer had just commenced. No hunting, no shooting to while away an idle hour. But Sir Alexander was as fond of old Izaak Walton's gentle craft, as that accomplished piscator, and we often rose at early dawn to stroll through the dewy pastures to the stream which crossed the park, which abounded with trout, and I soon became an excellent angler, hooking my fish in the most scientific manner.

When the days were not propitious for our sport, I accompanied Sir Alexander in his rides, in visiting his model farms, examining the progress of his crops, the making of hay, the improved breeds of sheep and cattle, and all such healthy and rural employments, in which he took a patriarchal delight.

Margaretta generally accompanied us on these expeditions. She was an excellent equestrian, and managed her high-bred roan with much skill and ease, never disturbing the pleasure of the ride by nervous or childish fears.

"Madge is a capital rider!" would the old Baronet exclaim. "I taught her myself. There is no affectation—no show-off airs in her riding. She does that as she does everything else, in a quiet, natural way."

The enjoyment of our country life was seldom disturbed by visitors. All the great folks were in London; the beauties of nature possessing far less attractions for them than the sophisticated gaieties of the season in town. If his youth had been dissipated, Sir Alexander courted retirement in age, and was perfectly devoted to the quiet happiness of a domestic life.

Margaretta, who shared all his tastes, and whose presence appeared necessary to his existence, had spent one season in London, but cared so little for the pleasures of the metropolis, that she resisted the urgent entreaties of her female friends to accompany them to town a second time.

"I hate London, Cousin Geoffrey. There is no room in its crowded scenes for nature and truth. Every one seems intent upon acting a lie, and living in defiance of their reason and better feelings. I never could feel at home there. I mistrusted myself and every one else, and never knew what true happiness was, until I returned to the unaffected simplicity of a country life."

These sentiments were fully reciprocated by me, who had passed, within the smoky walls of the huge metropolis the most unhappy period of my life.

Same hours, every day, were devoted by Sir Alexander to business, during which he was closely closeted with Mr. Hilton, his steward, and to disturb him at such times was regarded by him as an act of high treason.

During these hours, Margaretta and I were left to amuse ourselves in the best manner we could. She was a fine pianist. I had inherited my father's passion for music, and was never tired of listening to her while she played. If the weather was unfavourable for a ride or stroll in the Park, I read aloud to her, while she painted groups of flowers from nature, for which she had an exquisite taste. The time fled away only too fast, and this mingling of amusement and mental occupation was very delightful to me, whose chief employment for years had been confined to musty parchments in a dull, dark office.

Our twilight rambles through the glades of the beautiful park, at that witching hour when both eye and heart are keenly alive to sights and sounds of beauty, possessed for me the greatest charm.

I loved—but only as a brother loves—the dear, enthusiastic girl, who leaned so confidingly on my arm, whose glorious eyes, lighted up from the very fountain of passion and feeling, were raised to mine as if to kindle in my breast the fire of genius which emanated from her own.

Her vivid imagination, fostered in solitude, seized upon everything bright and beautiful in nature, and made it her own.

"The lips of song burst open

And the words of fire rushed out."

At such moments it was impossible to regard Margaretta with indifference. I could have loved, nay, adored, had not my mind been preoccupied with a fairer image.

Margaretta was too great a novice in affairs of the heart, to notice the guarded coolness of my homage. My society afforded her great pleasure, and she wanted the common-place tact of her sex to disguise it from me.

Dear, lovely, confiding Margaretta, how beautiful does your simple truth and disinterested affection appear, as I look back through the long vista of years, and find in the world so few who resemble thee!

Towards the close of a hot day in June we visited the fragrant fields of new-mown hay, and Margaretta tired herself by chasing a pair of small, coquettish blue butterflies, who hovered along the hedge, which bounded the dusty highway, like living gems, and not succeeding in capturing the shy things, she proposed leaving the road, and returning home through the Park.

"With all my heart," said I. "We will rest under your favourite beech, while you, dear Madge, sing with your sweet voice, the

"Drowsy world to rest."

We crossed a stile, and entered one of the broad, green arcades of the glorious old Park.

For some time we reposed upon the velvet sward, beneath Margaretta's favourite tree. The slanting red beams of the setting sun scarcely forced their way through the thickly interlaced boughs of the forest. The sparkling wavelets of the river ran brawling at our feet, fighting their way among the sharp rocks that opposed a barrier to their downward course. We bathed our temples in the cool, clear waters. Margaretta forgot the dusty road, the independent blue butterflies, and her recent fatigue.

"There is no music after all like the music of nature, Geoffrey," she said, untying her straw bonnet, and throwing it on the grass beside her, while she shook a shower of glossy black ringlets back from her small oval face.

"Not that it is the instrument, but the soul that breathes through it, which makes the music. And Nature, pouring her soul into these waves, and stirring with her plaintive sighs these branches above us, awakens sounds which find an echo in the heart of all her children, who remain true to the teachings of the divine mother." Then turning suddenly to me, she said, "Geoffrey, do you sing?"

"To please myself. I play upon the flute much better than I sing. During the last half year I remained with my uncle I took lessons of an excellent master, and having a good ear, and being passionately fond of music, I gained considerable proficiency. I had been an amateur performer for years."

"And you never told me one word of this before."

"I did not wish to display all my trifling stock of accomplishments at once," said I, with a smile. "Those who possess but little are wise to reserve a small portion of what they have. You shall test its value the next rainy day."

"In the absence of the flute, Geoffrey, you must give me a song. A song that harmonizes with this witching hour and holiday time o' the year."

"Then it must necessarily be a love song," said I; "youth and spring being the best adapted to inspire the joyousness of love."

"Call not love joyous, Geoffrey; it is a sad and fearful thing to love. Love that is sincere is a hidden emotion of the heart; it shrinks from vain laughter, and is most eloquent when silent, or only revealed by tears."

I started, and turned an anxious gaze upon her pale, spiritual face.

What right had I to be jealous of her? I who was devoted to another. Yet jealous I was, and answered rather pettishly:

"You talk feelingly, fair cousin, as if you had experienced the passion you describe. Have you tasted the bitter sadness of disappointed love?"

"I did not say that." And she blushed deeply. "You chose to infer it."

I did not reply. The image of Harrison rose in my mind. For the first time I saw a strong likeness between them. Such a likeness as is often found between persons who strongly assimilate—whose feelings, tastes, and pursuits are the same.

Was it possible that she had loved him? I was anxious to find out if my suspicions were true; and without any prelude or apology commenced singing a little air that Harrison had taught me, both music and words being his own.

SONG.

I loved you long and tenderly,
   I urged my suit with tears;
But coldly and disdainfully
   You crushed the hope of years.
I gazed upon your glowing cheek,
   I met your flashing eye;
The words I strove in vain to, speak
   Were smothered in a sigh.

I swore to love you faithfully,
   Till death should bid us part;
But proudly and reproachfully,
   You spurned a loyal heart.
Despair is bold—you turned away,
   And wished we ne'er had met,
Through many a long and weary day
   That parting haunts me yet.
Nor think that chilling apathy,
   Can passion's tide repress—
Ah, no! with fond idolatry,
   I would not love thee less.
Your image meets me in the crowd,
   Like some fair beam of light,
That bursting through its sombre cloud
   Makes glad the brow of night.
Then turn my hard captivity,
   Nor let me sue in vain,
Whilst with unshaken constancy,
   I seek your feet again.
One smile of thine can cheer the heart,
   That only beats to be
United, ne'er again to part—
   My life! my soul!—from thee.

  I sang my best, and was accounted by all the young men of my acquaintance, to have a fine manly voice. But I was not rewarded by a single word or encouraging smile.

  Margaretta's head was bowed upon her hands, and tears were streaming fast through her slender fingers.

"Margaret, dearest Margaret!" for in speaking to her, I always dropped the Italianized termination of her name. "Are you ill. Do speak to me."

She still continued to weep.

"I wish I had not sung that foolish song."

"It was only sung too well, Geoffrey." And she slowly raised her head and put back the hair from her brow. "Ah, what sad, what painful recollections does that song call up. But with these, you have nothing to do. I will not ask you how you became acquainted with that air; but I request as a great favour, that you will never sing or play it to me again."

She relapsed into silence, which I longed to break but did not know how. At length she rose from the bank on which we had been seated, resumed her bonnet, and expressed a wish to return to the Hall.

"The night has closed in very fast," said she, "or is the gloom occasioned by the shadow of the trees?"

"It is only a few minutes past seven," I replied, looking at my watch. "The hay-makers have not yet left their work." We had followed the course of the stream, on our homeward path, and now emerged into an open space in the Park. The sudden twilight which had descended upon us was caused by a heavy pile of thunder clouds which hung frowning over the woods, and threatened to overtake us before we could reach the Hall.

"How still and deep the waters lie," said Margaretta. "There is not a breath of wind to ruffle them or stir the trees. The awful stillness which precedes a storm inspires me with more dread, than when it launches forth with all its terrific powers."

"Hark! There's the first low peal of thunder, and the trees are all trembling and shivering in the electric blast which follows it. How sublimely beautiful, is this magnificent war of elements."

"It is very true, dear cousin, but if you stand gazing at the clouds, we shall both get wet."

"Geoffrey," said Margaretta, laughing, "there is nothing poetical about you."

"I have been used to the commonest prose all my life, Madge. But here we are at the fishing-house: we had better stow ourselves away with your father's nets and tackles until this heavy shower is over."

No sooner said than done. We crossed a rustic bridge which spanned the stream, and ascending a flight of stone steps, reached a small rough-cast building, open in front, with a bench running round three sides of it, and a rude oak table in the middle, which was covered with fishing-rods, nets, and other tackle belonging to the gentle craft.

From this picturesque shed Sir Alexander, in wet weather, could follow his favourite sport, as the river ran directly below, and it was considered the best spot for angling, the water expanding here into a deep still pool, much frequented by the finny tribes.

We were both soon seated in the ivy-covered porch, the honey-suckle hanging its perfumed tassels, dripping with the rain, above our heads, while the clematis and briar-rose gave out to the shower a double portion of delicate incense.

The scene was in unison with Margaretta's poetical temperament. She enjoyed it with her whole heart; her beautiful eyes brimful of love and adoration.

The landscape varied every moment. Now all was black and lowering; lightnings pierced with their arrowy tongues the heavy foliage of the frowning woods, and loud peals of thunder reverberated among the distant hills; and now a solitary sunbeam struggled through a rift in the heavy cloud, and lighted up the gloomy scene with a smile of celestial beauty.

Margaretta suddenly grasped my arm; I followed the direction of her eye, and beheld a tall female figure, dressed in deep mourning, pacing too and fro on the bridge we had just crossed. Her long hair, unconfined by cap or bandage, streamed in wild confusion round her wan and wasted features, and regardless of the pelting of the pitiless storm, she continued to hurry backwards and forwards, throwing her hands into the air, and striking her breast like one possessed.

"Who is she?" I whispered.

"The wreck of all that once was beautiful," sighed Margaretta, "It is Alice Mornington, the daughter of one of my father's tenants."

"Alice Mornington! Good Heavens! is that poor mad woman Alice Mornington?"

Margaretta looked surprised.

"Do you know this poor girl?"

I felt that I had nearly betrayed myself, and stammered out, "Not personally; I know something of her private history, which I heard accidentally before I came here."

"Geoffrey, no sister ever loved another more devotedly than I loved that poor girl—than I love her still. After she forsook the path of virtue, my father forbade me having the least intercourse with her. My heart bleeds to see her thus. I cannot stand calmly by and witness her misery. Stay here, while I go and speak to her."

With noiseless tread she glided down the stone steps, and gained the bridge. The quick eye of the maniac (for such she appeared to be) however, had detected the movement, and with a loud shriek she flung herself into the water.

To spring to the bank, to plunge into the stream, and as she rose to the surface, to bear the wretched girl to the shore, was but the work of a moment. Brief as the time was that had elapsed between the rash act and her rescue, she was already insensible, and with some difficulty I succeeded in carrying her up the steep steps to the fishing-house. It was some seconds before suspended animation returned, and when at length the large blue eyes unclosed, Alice awoke to consciousness on the bosom of the fond and weeping Margaretta.

"Oh, Miss Moncton!" sobbed the poor girl, "why did you save me—why did you recall me to a life of misery—why did you not let me die, when the agony of death was already over?"

"Dear Alice!" said Margaret, soothingly, "what tempted you to drown yourself?"

"I was driven to desperation by the neglect and cruelty of those whom I love best on earth."

"Do not reproach me, dear Alice," said Margaret, almost choking with emotion. "It is not in my nature to desert those I love. My heart has been with you in all your sorrows, but I dared not disobey my father."

"Oh, Miss Moncton, it was not of you I spoke. I could not expect you to countenance one whom the whole neighbourhood joined to condemn. If others had only treated me half as well, I should not have been reduced to such straits."

"Alice, you must not stay here in this sad state. You will get your death. Lean on my arm. I will take you home."

"Home! I have no home. I dare not go home. *She* is there! and she will taunt me with this, and drive me mad again."

"Then come to the Hall, Alice; I will talk to you there, and no one shall hear us but your own Margaret."

"God bless you! Miss Moncton, for all your kindness. It would, indeed, be a great relief to tell you all the grief which fills my heart. Yes, I will go with you to-night. The morrow may take care of the things which belong to it. Now, or never. There may be no to-morrow on earth for me."

"Cheer up, poor heart! There may be happiness in store for you yet," said Margaret.

"For me?" and Alice looked up with an incredulous smile; so sad, so dreary, it was enough to make you weep, that wild glance passing over her wan features. "Oh, never again for me."

She suffered herself to be led between us to the Hall; Margaret directing me by a path which led through the gardens to a private entrance at the back of the house. Alice was completely exhausted by her former violence. I had to put my arm round her slender waist, to support her up the marble stair-case. I left her with Margaret, at her chamber-door, and retired to my own apartment, to change my wet clothes.

Miss Moncton did not come down to tea.

Sir Alexander was in the fidgets about her. "Where's Madge? What the deuce is the matter with the girl? She went out with you, Geoffrey, as fresh as a lark. I will hold you responsible for her non-appearance."

I thought it best to relate what had happened. He looked very grave.

"A sad business! A very sad business! I wish Madge would keep her hands clear of that girl. I am sorry for her, too. But you know, Geoffrey, we cannot set the opinion of the world entirely at defiance. And what a man can do with impunity, a young lady must not."

"Miss Moncton has acted with true Christian charity, sir. It is sad that such examples are so rare."

"Don't think I blame Madge, Geoffrey. She is a dear, good girl, a little angel. But it is rather imprudent of her to bring the mistress of Theophilus home to the house. What will Mrs. Grundy say?"

"Margaret has no Mrs. Grundies," said I, rather indignantly. "She will not admit such vulgar, common-place wretches into her society. To the pure in heart all things are pure."

"Well done! young champion of dames. You will not suffer Margaretta to be blamed without taking her part, I see."

"Particularly, sir, when I know and feel that she is in the right."

"She and I must have a serious talk on this subject to-morrow, however. In the meantime, Geoffrey, bring here the chess-board, and let us get through a dull evening in the best way we can."

CHAPTER V.

A DISCOVERY.

The next morning I received from Margaretta, a circumstantial detail of what had passed between Alice and her on the previous evening. "After I undressed and got her to bed, she fell into a deep sleep, which lasted until midnight. I was reading by the table, not feeling at all inclined to rest. Hearing her moving, I went to her, and sat down on the bed, and asked how she felt herself.

"'Better in mind, Miss Moncton, but far from well. My head aches badly, and I have a dull pain in my chest.'

"'You have taken cold, Alice. I must send for the doctor.'

"'Oh! no, no. He could do me no good; mine is a malady of the heart. If my mind were at ease, I should be quite well. I do not wish to get well. The sooner I die the better.'

"'Alice, you must not talk so. It is very sinful.'

"'You are right—I am a great sinner. I know it only too well. But I cannot repent. All is dark here,' and she laid her hand upon her head. 'I cannot see my way through this thick darkness—this darkness which can be felt. You know, Miss Moncton, what the Bible says "The light of the wicked shall be put out in obscure darkness." My light of life has been extinguished, and the night of eternal darkness has closed over me.'

"'We must pray to God, Alice, to enlighten this awful darkness.'

"'Pray!—I cannot pray. I am too hard—too proud to pray. God has forsaken and left me to myself. If I could discern one ray of light—one faint glimmer only, I might cherish hope.'

"There was something so truly melancholy, in this description of the state of her mind, Geoffrey, that I could not listen to her with dry eyes.

"Alice, for her part, shed no tears, but regarded my emotions with a look of mingled pity and surprise, while the latent insanity, under which I am sure she is labouring, kindled a glow on her death-pale face. Rising slowly in the bed, she grasped my arm—

"'Why do you weep?' said she. 'Do you dare to think me guilty of that nameless crime? Margaretta Moncton, you should know me better. Don't you remember the ballad we once learned to repeat, when we were girls together?

"'Not mine to scowl a guilty eye,

   Or bear the brand of shame;

  Oh, God! to brook the taunting look

   Of Fillan's wedded dame.

"'But the lady bore the brand in spite of all her boasting. But I do not. I am a wife—*His* lawful wedded wife, and my boy was no child of shame, and he dare not deny it. And yet,' she continued, falling back upon her pillow, and clutching the bed-clothes in her convulsive grasp, '*he* spurned me from him —*me*, his wife—the mother of his child. Yes, Miss Moncton, spurned me from his presence, with hard words and bitter taunts. I could have borne the loss of his love, for I have long ceased to respect him. But this—this has maddened me.'

"I was perfectly astonished at this unexpected disclosure. Seeing doubt expressed in my face, she grew angry and vehement.

"'It is true. Why do you doubt my word? I scorn to utter a falsehood. When, Miss Moncton, did I ever during our long friendship deceive you?'

"'Never, Alice. But your story seemed improvable. Like you, I am in the habit of speaking fearlessly my mind.'

"She drew from her bosom a plain gold ring, suspended by a black ribbon round her neck.

"'With this ring we were married in Moncton Church. Our banns were published there, in your father's hearing, but he took no heed of the parties named. I have the certificate of my marriage, and Mr. Selden, who married us under the promise of secresy, can prove the truth of what I say. The marriage was private, because Theophilus was afraid of incurring his father's anger.'

"'And what has become of your child, Alice?'

"'He is dead,' she said, mournfully. 'He caught cold, during a long journey to London, which I undertook unknown to my grandmother, in the hope of moving the hard heart of my cruel husband. It was of no earthly use. I lost my child, and the desolate heart of the forsaken, is now doubly desolate.'

"The allusion to her baby seemed to soften the iron obstinacy of her grief, and she gave way to a passionate burst of tears. This, I have no doubt, tranquillized her mind. She grew calmer and more collected—consented to take some refreshments, and then unfolded to me at length, the tale of her wrongs.

"Oh, Geoffrey! what a monster that Theophilus Moncton must be. I may be wrong to say so, but I almost wish that poor Alice were not his wife, and so will you, after you have heard all that I have to tell you. Theophilus, it appears, from her statements, took a fancy to Alice, when she was a mere child, and his passion strengthened for her at every visit he subsequently paid to the Hall. After using every inducement to overcome her integrity, rather than lose his victim, he proposed a private marriage. This gratified the ambition of the unfortunate girl, who knew, that in case of my father dying without male issue, her lover would be the heir of Moncton. She was only too glad to close with his offer, and they were married in the parish church by the Rev. Mr. Selden, all the parties necessary to the performance of the ceremony being sworn or bribed to secresy.

"For a few months Theophilus lavished on his young bride great apparent affection, and at this period his visits to the Hall were very frequent.

"Alice, who had always been treated like a sister by me, now grew pert and familiar. This alteration in her former respectful manner greatly displeased my father. 'These Morningtons,' he said, 'are unworthy of the kindness we have bestowed upon them, and like all low people, when raised above their station, they become insolent and familiar.'

"Rumour had always ascribed young Moncton's visits to the Hall, to an attachment he had formed for me. The gossips of the village changed their tone, and his amour with Alice became the scandal of the day.

"My father having ascertained that there was some truth in these infamous reports, sent me to spend my first winter in London, with Lady Gray, my mother's only sister, and told Dinah North that her granddaughter for the future would be considered as a stranger by his family. I wrote to Alice from London, telling her that I could not believe the evil things said of her; and begged her, as she valued my love and friendship, to lose no time in clearing up the aspersions cast upon her character.

"To my earnest and affectionate appeal, she returned no answer, and all intercourse between us ceased. Three months after this, she became a mother, and my father forbade me to mention her name.

"It appears, that from this period she saw little of her husband; that he, repenting bitterly of his sudden marriage, treated her with coldness and neglect.

"Dinah North, who was privy to her marriage, took a journey to London, to try and force Mr. Moncton to acknowledge her granddaughter as his son's wife; in case of his refusal threatening to expose conduct of his which would not bear investigation. Dinah failed in her mission—and my dear father, pitying the condition of the forlorn girl, sought himself an interview with Mr. Moncton on her behalf, in which he begged your uncle to use his influence with Theophilus, to make her his wife. The young man had been sent abroad, and Mr. Moncton received my father's proposition with indignation and contempt, and threatened to disinherit Theophilus if he dared to take such a step without his knowledge and consent.

"In the meanwhile, the unfortunate Alice, withering beneath the blighting influence of hope deferred, and unmerited neglect, lost her health, her beauty, and by her own account, at times her reason. Hearing that her husband had returned to England, she wrote to him a letter full of forgiveness, and breathing the most devoted affection; and told him of the birth of his son, whom she described, with all a mother's doting love.

"To this letter she received, after a long and torturing delay, the following unfeeling answer. She gave me this precious document.

"Read it, Geoffrey. It puts me into a fever of indignation; I cannot read it a second time."

I took the letter from her hand.

How well I knew that scrupulously neat and feminine specimen of caligraphy. It was an autograph worthy of Queen Elizabeth, so regularly was each letter formed, the lines running in exact parallels; no flutter of the heart causing the least deviation from the exact rule. It ran as follows:

> "Why do you continue to trouble me with letters which are not worth the postage? I hate to receive them, and from this time forward will return them unopened.
>
> "Your best policy is to remain quiet, or I will disown the connection between us, and free myself from your importunity by consigning you to a mad-house.
>
> "T—— M——."

"Unfeeling scoundrel!" I exclaimed; "surely this *affectionate* billet must have destroyed the last spark of affection in the breast of the unhappy girl."

"Women are strange creatures, Geoffrey, and often cling with most pertinacity to those who care little for their regard, while they take a perverse pleasure in slighting those who really love them—so it is with Alice. The worse he treated her, the more vehemently she clung to him. To make a final appeal to his callous heart she undertook the journey to London alone, with her baby in her arms, and succeeded under a feigned name in getting admittance to her husband.

"You know the result. He spurned the wife and child from his presence. The infant was taken sick on its homeward journey, and died shortly after she reached her grandmother's cottage; and she, poor creature, will soon follow it to the grave, for I am convinced that she is dying of a broken heart."

Margaret was quite overcome with this sad relation. Wiping the tears from her eloquent black eyes, and looking me sadly in the face, she said, with great earnestness:

"And now, Geoffrey, what can we do to serve her?"

"Inform Sir Alexander of these particulars. Let him obtain from Alice the legal proofs of her marriage, and force this base Theophilus—this disgrace to the name of a man, and of Moncton, to acknowledge her publicly as his wife. In the meanwhile, I will write to her brother, and inform him of this important discovery."

"Her brother!" and Margaretta turned as pale as death; "what do you know of Philip Mornington?"

"He is my friend—my dearest, most valued friend."

"Thank God he is alive!"

"And likely to live," said I, leading her to a chair; for we had been standing during our long conversation in the deep recess of the library window. "Margaret, will you be offended if I ask you one question?"

"Not in the least, cousin."

"And will you answer me with your usual candour?"

"Why should you doubt it, Geoffrey?" said she, trembling with agitation.

"Do you love Philip Mornington?"

"I do, Geoffrey—I have loved him from a child, but not in the way you mean—not such love as a girl feels for her lover. I could not think of him for one moment as my husband. No, it is a strange interest I feel in his destiny: I feel as if he were a part of me, as if I had a natural right to love him. He is so like my father, only milder and less impetuous, that I have thought it possible that he might be his natural son—and if so, my brother."

What a relief was this declaration to my mind. I could not for a moment doubt its sincerity, and I rejoiced that the dear tender-hearted creature before me, was not likely to wreck her peace in loving one whom she could not wed. Yet, that she did love some one I felt certain; and though I dared not prosecute the inquiry, it was a problem that I was very anxious to solve.

I left my fair cousin, to write a long letter to George Harrison, in which I duly informed him of all that had taken place since I left London.

CHAPTER VI.
MY SECOND INTERVIEW WITH DINAH NORTH.

An hour had scarcely elapsed, when I received a message from Miss Moncton, requesting my presence in the drawing-room, where I found her engaged in an earnest conversation with Alice, who looked more like a resuscitated corpse, than a living creature; so pale and death-like were her beautiful features.

She held out her hand, as I approached the sofa on which she was reclining; and thanked me in low and earnest tones for saving her life. There was an expression of pride, almost aristocratical, on her finely cut lips, which seemed to contradict the gratitude she expressed.

"I was not in my right mind, Mr. Geoffrey; no one is, I have read and been told, who makes an attempt upon his own life. I had suffered a great calamity, and wanted moral courage to bear it. I trust God will forgive me."

I told her that I deeply sympathized with her unfortunate situation, and would gladly do anything in my power to serve her.

"That is more than Theophilus would do for you. If there is a person whom he hates more than me, it is yourself. You can serve me very materially. Miss Moncton tells me that you know my brother Philip intimately."

I nodded assent.

"Write to him, and tell him from me, how sincerely I repent my past conduct to him—that I am not quite the guilty creature he took me for; though swayed by minds more daringly wicked to commit evil. Tell him not to avenge my wrongs on Theophilus. There is one in heaven who will be my Avenger—who never lets the thoroughly bad escape unpunished; and tell him," and she drew a deep sigh—"that Alice Moncton died blessing him."

"Shall I go to London, and bring him down to see you?"

"No, no!" she cried, in evident alarm, "he must not be seen in this neighbourhood."

"That would be bringing the dead to life," said I, pointedly. She gave me a furtive look.

"Yes, Alice, Philip told me that dreadful story. I do not wonder at your repugnance to his coming here; and were it not for your share in the business, I would commit that atrocious woman to take her trial at the next assizes."

"Horrible!" muttered Alice, hiding her face in the sofa pillows. "I did not think that Philip would betray me, after all I did to save his life."

"Your secret is safe with me. I would to God, that other family secrets known to you and Dinah were in my keeping."

"I wish they were, Mr. Geoffrey, for I have too much upon my conscience, overburdened as it is with the crimes of others. But I cannot tell you many things important for you to know, for my lips are sealed with an oath too terrible to be broken."

"Then I must go to Dinah," I said, angrily, "and wrest the truth from her."

Alice burst into a wild laugh: "Rack and faggot would not do it, if she were determined to hold her tongue; nay, she would suffer that tongue to be torn out of her head, before she would confess a crime, unless indeed she were goaded on by revenge. Listen, Mr. Geoffrey, to the advice of a dying woman. Leave Dinah North to God and her own conscience. Before many months are over, her hatred to Robert Moncton and his son will tear the reluctant secret from her. Had my son lived," another heavy sigh, "it would have been different. Her ambition, like my love, has become dust and ashes."

"Alice," said I, solemnly, "you have no right to withhold knowledge which involves the happiness of others; even for your oath's sake."

"It may be so, but that oath involves an eternal penalty which I dare not bring upon my soul."

"God can absolve all rash vows."

"Ay, those who believe in Him, who love and trust Him. I believe, simply because I fear. But love and trust—alas, the comfort, the assurance which springs from faith, was never felt by me."

"Dinah may die, and the secret may perish with her," cried I, growing desperate to obtain information on a subject of such vital importance to my friend—perhaps to me.

"That is nothing to me," she replied, coldly.

"Selfish, ungenerous woman!"

She smiled scornfully. "The world, and your family especially, have given me great encouragement to be liberal."

"Is Philip your brother?" cried I, vehemently, determined to storm the secret out of her.

"What is that to you? Yet, perhaps, if the truth were told, you would be the first to wish it buried in oblivion."

There was a lurking fire in her eye as she said this, which startled me.

"Do you wish to prosecute the inquiry?" added she, with the bitter smile which made her face, though beautiful, very repulsive.

A glance of contempt was my sole answer.

"Well, once for all, I will tell you, Mr. Geoffrey, lawyer though you be, that your cross-questioning is useless. What I know about you and yours shall remain unknown, as far as I am concerned; and shall go down with me to the grave. The memory of my mother is too dear to me for any words of yours to drag from me the trust she reposed in me. You have had your answer. Go—I wish to be alone."

In vain I argued, entreated, and even threatened. There was too much of the leaven of Old Dinah in her granddaughter's character for her to listen to reason.

She became violent and obstinate, and put an end to this strange conference by rising, and abruptly leaving the room. I looked after her with feelings less tinctured with compassion than annoyance and contempt.

"Forgive her! Geoffrey," said Margaretta, who had listened in silent astonishment to the conversation; "her reason is disordered; she does not know what she says."

"The madness of wickedness," I said, sharply. "She is as wide awake as a fox. It may seem harsh to say so, but I feel little pity for her. She is artful and selfish in the extreme, and deserves her fate. Just review, for a moment, her past life."

"It will not bear investigation, Geoffrey. Yet, with all these faults, I loved her so fondly—love her still, and will never desert her while a hope remains, that through my instrumentality her mind may be diverted to the contemplation of better things."

"She is not worthy of the trouble you take about her," said I, shrugging my shoulders. "Have you informed your father of her marriage with Theophilus?"

"Yes, and he was astonished. Theophilus was the last person in the world, he thought, who would commit himself in that way. Papa said, that he would write to Robert Moncton, and make a statement of the facts. I could almost pity him; this news will throw him into such a transport of rage."

"When Robert Moncton feels the most, he says little. He acts with silent, deadly force. He seldom speaks. He will curse Theophilus in his heart, but speak fair of him to his enemies. I am anxious to know how all this will end."

"My father wanted to see you in the library," said Margaretta. "Your conversation with Alice put it entirely out of my head."

I found Sir Alexander seated at a table, surrounded with papers. If there was one thing my good old friend hated more than another, it was writing letters. "Wise men speak—fools write their thoughts," was a favourite saying of his. He flung the pen pettishly from him as I entered the room.

"Zounds! Geoffrey. I cannot defile paper with writing to that scoundrel. I will see him myself. Who knows, but in the heat of his displeasure, he may say something that will afford a clue to unravel his treachery towards yourself. At all events, I am determined to make the experiment."

"He will make no sign. Robert Moncton never betrays himself."

"To think that his clever Theophilus could make such a low marriage; not but that the girl is far too good for him, and I think the degradation is entirely on her side."

"The pair are worthy of each other," said I.

"You are unjust to Alice, Geoffrey. The girl was a beauty, and so clever, till he spoilt her."

"The tiger is a beautiful animal, and the fox is clever; but we hate the one, and despise the other."

The Baronet gave me a curious look.

"How came you to form this character of the girl?"

"Partly from observation; partly from some previous knowledge, obtained from a reliable source, before I left London. But what of this journey," said I, anxious to turn the conversation. "Do you seriously contemplate again going up to town?"

"It is already decided. I have ordered the carriage to be at the door by eight to-morrow morning. I do not ask you to accompany me, Geoffrey. I have business cut out for you during my absence. You must start to-morrow for Derbyshire, and visit the parish in which your grandfather resided for many years as curate, under the Rev. James Brownson; and where your mother was born. I will supply the necessary funds for the journey."

"And the object of this visit?" cried I, eagerly.

"To take lodgings in ———, or in the neighbourhood, and, under a feigned name, prosecute inquiries respecting your mother's marriage. There must still be many persons living to whom Ellen Rivers and her father were well-known, who might give you much valuable information respecting her elopement with your father, and what was said about it by the gossips at the time. If you find the belief general that they were married, ascertain the church in which the ceremony was said to have been performed—the name of the clergyman who officiated, and the witnesses who were present. All these particulars are of the greatest importance for us to know. Take the best riding-horse in the stable, and if your money fails you, draw upon me for more. You may adopt, for the time being, my mother's family name, and: call yourself Mr. Tremain, to which address, all letters from the Hall will be sent. Should Robert Moncton drop any hints, which can in any way further the object of your search, I will not fail to write you word. We will, if you please, start at the same hour to-morrow; each on our different mission; and may God grant us success, and a happy meeting. And, now, you may go and prepare for your adventure."

I had long wished to prosecute this inquiry. Yet, now the moment had arrived, I felt loath to leave the Hall.

The society and presence of Margaretta had become necessary to my happiness. Yet inconsistently enough, I fancied myself desperately in love with Catherine Lee: I never suspected that my passion for the one was ideal—the first love of a boy; while that for the latter, was real and tangible.

How we suffer youth and imagination to deceive us in affairs of the heart! We love a name, and invest the person who bears it with a thousand perfections, which have no existence in reality. The object of our idolatry is not a child of nature, but a creation of fancy, fostered in solitude by ignorance and self-love. Marriages, which are the offspring of first-love, are proverbially unhappy from this very circumstance, which leads us to overrate, during the period of courtship, the virtues of the beloved in the most extravagant manner; and this species of adoration generally ends in disappointment—too often in disgust.

Boys and girls in their teens, are beings without much reflection. Their knowledge of character, with regard to themselves and others, is too limited and imperfect to enable them to make a judicious choice. They love the first person who pleases the eye and charms the fancy—for love is a matter of necessity at that age. Time divests their idol of all its imaginary perfections, and they feel, too late, that they have made a wrong choice. Though love may laugh at the cold maxims of prudence and reason, yet it requires the full exercise of both qualities to secure for any length of time domestic happiness.

I can reason calmly now, on this exciting subject. But I reasoned not calmly then. I was a creature of passion, and passionate impulses. The woman I loved had no fault in my eyes. To have supposed her liable to the common errors and follies of her sex would have been an act of treason against the deity I worshipped.

I retired to my chamber, and finished my letter to Harrison.

The day wore slowly away, as it always does when you expect any important event on the morrow.

The evening was bright and beautiful as an evening in June could well be. Margaretta had only been visible at dinner, her time having been occupied between Alice and making preparations for her father's journey. At tea, she looked languid and paler than usual, and when we rose from the table I proposed a stroll in the Park. She consented with a smile of pleasure, and we were soon wandering side by side beneath our favourite trees.

"You will feel very lonely during your father's absence, my little cousin?"

"Then you must exert all your powers of pleasing, Geoffrey, to supply his place."

"But I am going too: I leave Moncton at the same time, for an indefinite period."

"Worse and worse," and she tried to smile. It would not do. The tears were in her beautiful eyes. That look of tender inquiry caused a strange swelling at my heart.

"You will not forget me, Margaret?"

"Do you think it such an easy matter, that you deem it necessary to make such a request."

"I am but a poor relation, whom few persons would regard with other feelings than those of indifference. This I know is not the case with your excellent father and you. I shall ever regard both with gratitude and veneration—and I feel certain, that should we never meet again, I should always be remembered with affectionate kindness."

"You know not how deservedly dear you are to us both. How much we love you, Geoffrey—and I would fain hope that these sentiments are reciprocal."

Though this was said in perfect simplicity, the flushed cheek, and downcast eye, revealed the state of the speaker's heart, I felt—I knew—she loved me. But, madman that I was, out of mere contradiction, I considered myself bound by a romantic attachment, which had never been declared by word or sign, to Catherine Lee.

"You love me, dear Margaret," cried I, as I clasped her hand in mine, and kissed it with more warmth than the disclosure I was about to make, warranted.

"God knows! how happy this blessed discovery would have made me, had not my affections been pre-engaged."

A deep blush mantled over her face—she trembled violently as she gently drew her hand from mine—and answered with a modest dignity, which was the offspring of purity and truth.

"I will not deny, Geoffrey, that I love you. What you have said gives me severe pain. We are not accountable for our affections: I am sorry that I suffered my foolish heart to betray me. Yet, I must love you still, cousin," she said, weeping. "Your very misfortunes endear you to me. Forget this momentary weakness, and only think of me as a loving friend and kinswoman."

Mastering her feelings with a strong effort, she bade me good night, and slowly walked back to the Hall.

I was overwhelmed with confusion and remorse. I had wantonly sported with the affections of one of the gentlest and noblest of human beings, which a single hint, dropped as if accidentally, of a previous passion might have prevented.

Between Catherine and me, no words of love had been exchanged. She might be the love of another—might be a wife, for anything I knew to the contrary. I had neither seen nor heard anything regarding her for some months, I had sacrificed the peace and happiness of the generous, confiding Margaretta, to an idol, which might only exist in my own heated imagination.

Bitterly I cursed my folly when repentance came too late.

I was too much vexed and annoyed with myself to return to the Hall, and I rambled on until I found myself opposite to the fishing-house. The river lay before me gleaming in the setting sun. Everything around was calm, peaceful, and beautiful; but there was no rest, no peace in my heart.

As I approached the rustic bridge from which the wretched Alice had attempted suicide, I perceived a human figure seated on a stone on the bank of the river, in a crouching, listless attitude. This excited my curiosity, and catching at anything that might divert my thoughts from the unpleasant train in which they had been running for the last hour, I struck off the path I had been pursuing, which led directly to the public road, and soon reached the object in question.

Wrapped in an old grey mantle, with a red silk handkerchief tied over her head, her chin resting between her long bony hands, and her eyes shut, or bent intently on the ground, I recognized, with a shudder of aversion and disgust, the remarkable face of Dinah North.

Her grizzled locks had partly escaped from their bandage, and fell in thin, straggling lines over her low, wrinkled forehead. The fire of her deep-seated dark eyes was hidden beneath their drooping lids, and she was muttering to herself some strange unintelligible gibberish. She did not notice me until I purposely placed myself between her and the river which rolled silently and swiftly at her feet.

Without manifesting the least surprise at the unceremonious manner in which I had disturbed her reverie, she slowly raised her witch-like countenance, and for a few seconds surveyed me with a sullen stare. As if satisfied with my identity, she accosted me with the same sarcastic writhing of the upper lip, which on our first interview had given me the key to her character.

"You, too, are a Moncton, and like the rest of that accursed race, are fair and false. Your dark eyes all fire—your heart as cold as ice. Proud as Lucifer —inexorable as the grave; woe to those who put any trust in a Moncton! they are certain of disappointment—sure to be betrayed. Pass by, young sir, I have no doubt that you are like the rest of your kin. I wish them no good, but evil, so you had better not cross my path."

"Your hatred, Dinah, is more to be coveted than your friendship. To incur the first, augurs some good in the person thus honoured; to possess the last, would render us worthy of your curse."

"Ha, ha!" returned the grim fiend, laughing ironically, "your knowledge of the world has given you a bitter spirit. I wish you joy of the acquisition. Time will increase its acrimony. But I like your bluntness of speech, and prophesy from it that you are born to overcome the malignity of your enemies."

"And you," and I fixed my eyes steadily on her hideous countenance, "for what end were you born?"

"To be the curse of others," she answered, with a grim smile, which displayed those glittering white teeth within her faded, fleshless lips, which looked like a row of pearls in a Death's head; and there flashed from her swart eye a red light which made the blood curdle in my veins, as she continued in the same taunting strain—

"I have been of use, too, in my day and generation. I have won many souls, but not for heaven. I have served my master well, and shall doubtless receive my reward."

"This is madness, Dinah North, but without excuse. It is the madness of guilt."

"It is a quality I possess in common with my kind. The world is made up of madmen and fools. It is better to belong to the first than to the latter class—to rule, than to be ruled. Between those two parties the whole earth is divided. Knowledge is power, whether it be the knowledge of evil or of good. I heard that sentence when a girl; it never left my mind, and I have acted upon it through life."

"It must have been upon the knowledge of evil—as your deeds can too well testify."

"You have guessed right, young sir. By it, the devil lost heaven, but he gained hell. By it tyrants rule, and mean men become rich—virtue is overcome, and vice triumphs."

"And what have you gained by it?"

"Much: it has given me an influence in the world, which without it, never could have belonged to one of my degree. By it, I have swayed the destinies of those whom fortune had apparently placed beyond my reach. It has given me, Geoffrey Moncton, power over thee and thine, and at this very moment, the key of your future fortune is in my keeping."

"And your life in mine, vain boaster! The hour is at hand which shall make even a hardened sinner like you acknowledge that there is a righteous God who judges in the earth. I ask you not for the secret which you possess, and which, after all, may be a falsehood, in unison with the deceit and treachery that has marked your whole life—a lie, invented to extort money, or to gratify the spite of your malignant heart. The power which punishes the guilty and watches over the innocent, will vindicate the good name of which a wretch like you would fain deprive me."

"Don't be too sure of *celestial* aid," said she, with a sneer, "but, 'make to yourself friends of the mammon of unrighteousness,' as the wisest policy.

Flatter from your Uncle Robert the ill-gotten wealth that his dastardly son, Theophilus, shall never possess."

"This advice comes well from the sordid woman who sold her innocent grandchild to this same Theophilus, in the hope that she might enjoy the rank and fortune which belonged to the good and noble, and by this unholy act sacrificed the peace—perhaps the eternal happiness of that most wretched creature."

The countenance of the old woman grew dark—dark as night. She fixed upon me a wild, inquiring gaze.

"You speak of Alice. In the name of God, tell me what has become of her!"

"Upon one condition," said I, laying my hand upon her shoulder and whispering the words into her ear. "Tell me what has become of Philip Mornington."

"Ha!" said the old woman, trying to shake off my grasp; "what do you know of him?"

"Enough to hang you—something that the grave in the dark shrubbery can reveal."

"Has she told you *that*? The fool! the idiot! in so doing she betrayed herself."

"*She* told me nothing. The eye that witnessed the deed confided to me that secret. The earth will not conceal the stain of blood. Did you never hear that fact before? Is not my secret as good as yours, Dinah North? Are you willing to make an exchange?"

The old woman crouched herself together, and buried her face between her knees. Her hands opened and shut with a convulsive motion, as if they retained something in their grasp with which she was unwilling to part. At length, raising her head, she said in a decided manner:

"The law has lost in you a *worthy* member; but I accept the terms. Come to me to-morrow at nine o'clock."

"To-night, or never!"

"Don't try to force or bully me into compliance, young man. At my own time, and in my own way alone, will I gratify your curiosity."

"Well, be it so—to-morrow. I will meet you at the Lodge at nine to-morrow."

She rose from her seat; regarded me with the same withering glance and cutting smile, and gliding past me, vanished among the trees.

Exulting in my success, I exclaimed—"Thank God I shall know all to-morrow!"

CHAPTER VII.

AN EXPLANATION—DEPARTURE—DISAPPOINTMENT.

I was so elated with the unexpected result of my meeting with Dinah North, that it was not until I missed the fairy figure of my sweet cousin at the supper-table, that my mind reverted to the conversation that had passed between us in the Park.

"Where is Miss Moncton?" I asked of Sir Alexander, in a tone and manner which would have betrayed the agitation I felt, to a stranger.

"She is not well, Geoffrey, has a bad headache, or is nervous, I forget which, and begged to be excused joining us to-night. These little female complaints are never dangerous, so don't look alarmed. My girl is no philosopher, and this double parting affects her spirits. She will be all right again when you come back."

I sighed involuntarily. The provoking old man burst into a hearty laugh.

"I am likely to have a dull companion to-night, Geoffrey. Hang it! boy, don't look so dismal. Do you think that you are the only man who ever was in love? I was a young man once. Ay, and a fine young man too, or the world and the ladies told great stories, but I never could enact the part of a sentimental lover. Fill your glass and drive away care. Success to your journey. Our journeys, I might have said—and a happy meeting with little Madge."

I longed to tell Sir Alexander the truth, and repeat to him my conversation with his daughter. But I could not bear to mortify his pride, for I could not fail to perceive that he contemplated a union between us with pleasure, and was doing his best to encourage me to make a declaration of my attachment to Margaret.

I was placed in a most unfortunate predicament, and in order to drown my own miserable feelings, I drank more wine than usual, and gaining an artificial flow of spirits, amused my generous patron with a number of facetious stories and anecdotes, until the night was far advanced, and we both retired to rest.

My brain was too much heated with the wine I had drank to sleep, and after making several ineffectual efforts, I rose from my bed—relighted my candle, and dressing myself, sat down to my desk, and wrote a long letter to Margaretta, in which I informed her of my first meeting with Catherine Lee; the interest which her beauty had created in my heart—the romantic attachment I had formed for her, and which, hopeless as it was, I could not wholly overcome. I assured Margaretta, that I felt for herself, the greatest affection and esteem—that but for the remembrance of the first passion, the idea that she loved me would have made me the happiest of men. That if she would accept the heart I had to offer, divided as I felt it was with another, and my legitimacy could be established, my whole life should be devoted to her alone.

I ended this long candid confession, by relating verbatim my interview with Dinah North, and begged, if possible, that I might exchange a few words with her before leaving the Hall.

I felt greatly relieved by thus unburdening my mind. I had told the honest truth, without fear and without disguise; and I knew that she, who was the mirror of truth, would value my sincerity as it deserved.

The sun was scarcely up when I dispatched my letter, and before the early breakfast, that had been ordered previous to our departure, was ready, I received the following answer—

"My dear Cousin Geoffrey,

"Your invaluable letter has greatly raised you in my esteem; I cannot sufficiently admire the conscientious scruples which dictated it—and though we cannot meet as lovers, after the candid revelation you have confided to me, we may still remain, what all near relatives ought to be, firm and faithful friends.

"To you I can attach no blame whatever, and I feel proud that my affections, though fixed upon an object beyond their reach, were bestowed upon one so every way worthy of them.

"Let us therefore forget our private sorrows, and drown unavailing regrets in doing all we can to serve Philip and his sister. Farewell—with sincere prayers for the successful issue of your journey, believe me, now and ever, your faithful and loving friend,

"MARGARETTA."

"What a noble creature she is," said I, as I pressed the letter to my lips; "I am indeed unworthy of such a treasure."

Yet I felt happy at that moment; happy that she knew all—that I had not deceived her, but had performed an act of painful duty, though by so doing I had perhaps destroyed the brilliancy of my future prospects in life.

With mingled feelings of gratitude and pleasure I met my dear cousin at the breakfast-table. Her countenance, although paler than usual, wore a tranquil and even cheerful expression.

"Why, Madge, my darling," cried the Baronet, kissing her pale cheek, "you are determined to see the last of us: is your early rising in honour of Geoffrey or me?"

"Of both," she said, with her sweetest smile. "I never employ a proxy to bid farewell to my friends."

Several efforts were made at conversation during the meal, which proved eminently unsuccessful. The hour of parting came. The Baronet was safely stowed away into his carriage; the noble horses plunged forward, and the glittering equipage was soon lost among the trees. I lingered a moment behind.

"Dear Margaret, we part friends."

"The best of friends."

"God bless you! dearest and noblest of women," said I, faintly; for my lips quivered with emotion; I could scarcely articulate a word; "you have removed a load of anxiety from my heart. To have lost your friendship would have been a severer trial to me, than the loss of name or fortune."

"I believe you, Geoffrey. But never allude again to this painful subject, if you value my health and peace. We understand each other. If God wills it so, we may both be happy, though the attainment of it may not exactly coincide with our present wishes. Adieu! dear cousin. You have my heart-felt prayers for your success."

She raised her tearful eyes to mine. The next moment she was in my arms, pressed closely against my breast—a stifled sob—one kiss—one long lingering embrace—a heavy melancholy deep-drawn sigh, and she was gone.

I mounted my horse and rode quickly forward; my thoughts so occupied with Margaretta and that sad parting, that I nearly forgot the promised interview with Dinah North, until my proximity to the lodge brought it vividly to my remembrance.

Fastening my horse to the rustic railing which fronted the cottage, I crossed the pretty little flower-garden, and knocked rather impatiently at the door. My summons, though given in loud and authoritative tones, remained unanswered.

Again and again I applied my hand to the rusty iron knocker; it awoke no response from the tenant of the house. "She must be dead or out," said I, losing all patience; "I will stay here no longer," and lifting the latch, I very unceremoniously entered the cottage. All was silent within. The embers on the hearth were dead, and the culinary vessels were scattered over the floor. The white muslin curtains which shaded the rose-bound windows were undrawn. The door which led into the bedroom was open, the bed made and the room untenanted. It was evident that the old woman was not there. I called aloud:

"Dinah, Dinah North! Is any one within?"

No answer.

I proceeded to explore the rest of the dwelling. In the front room or parlour, the contents of a small chest of drawers had been emptied out on the floor, and some few articles of little value were strewn about. It was an evident fact, that the bird had flown; and all my high-raised expectations resolved themselves into air.

Whilst cursing the crafty old woman bitterly in my heart, my eye glanced upon a slip of paper lying upon a side table. I hastily snatched it up and read the following words traced in a bold hand:

> "Geoffrey Moncton, when next we meet, your secret and mine will be of equal value.
>
> "DINAH NORTH."

I was bitterly disappointed, and crushing the paper in my hand, I flung it as far from me as I could.

"Curse the old fiend! We shall yet meet. I will trace her to the utmost bounds of earth to bring her to justice."

I left the house in a terrible ill-humour, and remounting my horse, pursued my journey, to Derbyshire.

It was late on the evening of the second day, when I reached the little village over which my grandfather Rivers had exercised the pastoral office for nearly fifty years. The good man had been gathered to his fathers a few months before I was born. It was not without feeling a considerable degree of interest that I rode past the humble church, surrounded by its lofty screen of elms, and glanced at the greensward beneath whose daisy-sprinkled carpet, the

"Rude forefathers of the village slept."

The rain had fallen softly but perseveringly the whole day, and I was wet, hungry and tired. I hailed therefore the neat little inn, with its gay sign-board, white-washed walls and green window-blinds, as the most welcome and picturesque object which had met my sight for the last three hours.

"Stay all night, sir?" said the brisk lad, from whose helmet-like leathern cap the water trickled in the most obtrusively impertinent manner over his rosy, freckled face, as he ran forward to hold my horse. "Good accommodation for man and beast—capital beds, sir."

"Yes, yes," I replied, somewhat impatiently, as I threw him the reins and entered the brick passage of the inn. "Where is the master of the house?"

"No master, sir," returned the officious lad, following me. "The master be a missus, sir. Here she come."

"What's your pleasure?" said a very pretty woman, about thirty years of age, advancing from an inner room. She was dressed in widow's weeds, which became her very fair face amazingly, and led by the hand a rosy, curly-headed urchin, whose claims to general admiration were by no means contemptible. The mother and her lovely boy would have made a charming picture; and I forgot, while contemplating the originals, that I was wet and hungry.

With the quickness of her sex, Mrs. Archer perceived that she had made a favourable impression on her new guest. And putting back the luxuriant curls from the white brow of her boy, she remarked, with a sigh:

"He's young to be an orphan—poor child!"

"He is, indeed," I replied, kissing the little fellow, as I spoke; "and his mother far too young and pretty to remain long a widow."

"La! sir; you don't say so," said Mrs. Archer, smiling and blushing most becomingly. "And you standing all this while in the drafty, cold passage in your wet clothes. You can have a private room and a fire, sir."

"And a good supper, I hope," said I, laughing. "I have ridden fifty miles to-day, and I feel desperately hungry."

"You shall have the best the house affords. Pray, walk this way."

I followed my conductress into a neat little room. A fat country girl was on her knees before the grate striving to kindle the fire; but the wood was wet, and in spite of the girl's exertions, who was supplying with her mouth the want of a pair of bellows, the fire refused to burn.

"It's of no manner of use: no it isn't," said the girl. "I may blow till I bust, an' it won't kindle."

"Try again, Betty," said her mistress, encouragingly. "You were always a first-rate hand at raising the fire."

"But the wood warn't wet," returned the fat girl, discontentedly. "I can't make it burn when it won't."

And getting up from her fat knees she retreated, scowling alternately at me and the refractory fire.

The room looked cold and comfortless. The heavy rain dashed drearily against the narrow window-panes; and I inquired if I could not dry my wet clothes and eat my supper by the kitchen-fire.

"Oh! yes. If such a gentleman as you will condescend to enter my humble kitchen," was the reply.

I did condescend—heaven only knows how gladly; and soon found myself comfortably seated before an excellent fire, in company with a stout, red-faced, jolly old farmer, and a thin, weazel-faced, undersized individual, dressed in a threadbare suit of pepper and salt, who kept his hat on, and wore it on one side with a knowing swagger, talked big, and gave himself a thousand consequential airs.

This person I discovered to be the barber, and great politician of the village; who talked continually of King George and the royal family; of the king's ministers; the war in Rooshia, the burning of Moscow, and the destruction of that monster Bonyparty.

The farmer, who was no scholar, and looked upon him of the strop and razor as a perfect oracle, was treating him to a pot of ale, for the sake of the news; the barber paying twopence a week for the sight of a second-hand newspaper.

Mrs. Archer went softly up to the maker of perukes, and whispered something in his ear. He answered with a knowing nod, and without moving, stared me full in the face.

"Not an inch will I budge, Mrs. Archer. One man's money is as good as another man's money. No offence to the gemman, 'A man's a man for a' that.' That's what I call real independence, neighbour Bullock."

And his long, lean fingers descended upon the fat knee of the farmer with a whack that rang through the kitchen.

"Deuce take you! Sheldrake. I wish you'd just show it in some other way," said the farmer, rubbing his knee. "Why, man, your fingers are as long and as lean as a crow's claws, and as hard as your own block, and sting like whipcord. One would think that you had dabbled long enough in oil and pomatum, and such like messes, to make them as white as a lady's hand, and as soft as your own head."

"They have been made tough by handling such hard numskulls as yours, neighbour Bullock. That chin of yours, with its three days' growth of bristles, would be a fortune to a bricklayer, whilst it spoils my best razors, and never puts a penny into the pocket of the poor operator."

"*Operator!*" repeated the farmer, with a broad, quizzical grin, "is that your new-fangled name for a shaver? It's a pity you didn't put it on the board with the farrago of nonsense, by which you hope to attract the attention of all the fool bodies in the town."

"Don't speak disrespectfully of my sign, sir," quoth the little barber, waxing wroth. "My sign is an excellent sign—the admiration of the whole village; and let me tell you that it is not in *spite* and *envy* to put it down, let spite and envy try as hard as they can. The genius which suggested that sign is not destined to go unrewarded."

"Ha! ha! ha,!" roared the chewer of bacon.

"Mrs. Archer," said the offended shaver, turning to the pretty widow with an air of wounded dignity truly comic, "did you ever before hear a Bullock laugh like a hog?"

"Dang it! man, such conceit would make a cow caper a horn-pipe, or a Shelled Drake crow like a cock."

"I beg you, *Mister* Bullock, to take no liberties with my name, especially in the presence of the fair sex," bowing gracefully to Mrs. Archer, who was leaning upon the back of my chair, half suffocated with suppressed laughter.

"What are you quarrelling about, Sheldrake?" said the good-natured widow. "Bullock, can't you let his sign alone? It is something new, I hear—something in praise of the ladies."

"I was always devoted to the ladies," said the barber, "having expended the best years of my life in their service."

"Well, well, if so be that you call that powetry over your door a compliment to the women-folk, I'll be shot!" said the farmer. "Now, sir," turning to me, "you are a stranger, and therefore unprejudiced; you shall be judge. Come, barber, repeat your verses, and hear what the gemman says of them."

"With all my heart;" and flinging his shoulders back and stretching forth his right arm, the barber repeated, in a loud theatrical tone—

> "I, William, Sheldrake, shave for a penny,
>
> Ladies and gentlemen—there can't come too many—
>
> With heads and beards—I meant to say
>
> Those who've got none may keep away."

A hearty burst of laughter from us all greatly disconcerted the barber, who looked as ruefully at us as a stuck pig.

"You hairy monster!" quoth Mrs. Archer, "what do you mean by shaving the ladies? You deserve to be ducked to death in a tub of dirty suds. Beards, forsooth!" and she patted, with evident complacency, her round, white, dimpled chin; "who ever saw a woman with a beard? Did you take us all for Lapland witches? I wonder what our pretty young lady up at Elm Grove would say to your absurd verses."

"That is no secret to me, Mrs. Archer. I do know what she thinks of it. Miss Lee is a young lady of taste, and knows how to appreciate fine poetry, which is more than some folks, not a hundred miles off, does. She rode past my shop yesterday on horseback, and I saw her point to my sign with her riding-whip, and heard her say to the London chap that is allers with her, 'Is not that *capital*?'

"And he says, '*Capital!* If that does not draw custom to the shop, nothing will.' So now, neighbour Bullock, you may just leave off sneering at my sign."

"I did not think Miss Lee had been such a fool," said Bullock, "but there's no accounting for taste."

"Who is the gentleman that is staying at the Elms just now?" asked Mrs. Archer. "Do you know his name?"

"I've heard," said Suds, "but really I quite forget. It either begins with an M or an N."

"That's a wide landmark to sail by, Sheldrake. You might as well have added a P or a Q."

"Stop," said the barber, "I can give you a clue to it. Do you remember, Bullock, the name of the fine sporting gemman who ran off with Parson Rivers's daughter? I was a boy then, serving my time with Sam Strap."

I started from the contemplation of the fine well-grilled beef-steak which Mrs. Archer was dishing for my especial benefit.

"Well," said Sheldrake, "he is either a son or a nefy of his, and has the same name."

"The deuce he is! That was Moncton, if I mistake not. Yes, yes, Moncton was the name. I well remember it, for it was the means of our losing our good old pastor."

"How was that?" said I, trying to look indifferent.

"Why, sir, do you see. Mr. Rivers had been many years in the parish. He married my father and mother, and baptized me, when a babby. He did more than that. He married me to my old woman, when I was a man—but that was the worse job he ever done. Well, sir, as I was telling you. He was a good man and a Christian; but he had one little weakness. We have all our faults, sir. He loved his pretty daughter too well: wise men will sometimes play the fool, and 'tis a bad thing to make too much of woman-kind. Like servants they grow saucy upon it. They always gets the advantage, any how; and our old parson did pet and spoil Miss Ellen to her heart's content. There was some excuse too for him, for he was an old man and a widower. He had lost his wife and a large family. Parsons always have large families. My wife do say, that 'tis because they have nothing else to do. But I'se very sure, that I should find preaching and sermon-work hard enough."

"Lord! man, what a roundabout way you have of telling a story," cried Suds, who was impatient to hear his own voice again. "Get on a little quicker. Don't you see, the gemman's steak is a-getting cold—and he can't eat and listen to you at the same time, an art I learnt long ago."

"Mind your own business, Sheldrake," said the farmer: "I never trouble my head with the nonsense which is always frothing out of your mouth."

"Well, sir," turning again to me, "as I was saying; his wife and family had all died in the consumption, which made him so afraid of losing Miss Ellen, that he denied her nothing; and truly, she was as pretty a piece of God's workmanship as ever you saw—and very sweet-tempered and gentle, which beauties seldom are. I had the misfortune to marry a pretty woman, and I knows it to my cost. But I need not trouble you with my missus. It's bad enough to be troubled with her myself. So, sir, as I was telling you, there came a mighty fine gentleman down from London, to stay at the Elm Grove, with my old landlord Squire Lee, who's dead and gone. This Squire Lee was the son of old-Squire Lee."

"I dare say, Bullock, the gemman does not care a farthing whose son he was," cried the impatient barber. "You are so fond of genealogies, that it's a pity you don't begin with the last squire, and end with, 'which was the son of Seth, which was the son of Adam,' &c."

These interruptions were very annoying, as I was on the tenter-hooks to get out of the mountain of flesh, the head and tail of the story he found such difficulty in bringing forth.

"Pray go on with your story, friend," said I, very demurely, for fear of hurrying him into becoming more discursive, "I feel quite interested."

"Well, sir, this young man came to stay at the Grove, during the shooting-season; and he sees Miss Ellen at church, and falls desperately in love with her. This was all very natural. I was a youngster myself once, and a smart active chap, although I be clumsy enough now, and I remember feeling rather queerish, whenever I cast a sheep's eye into the parson's pew."

"But the young lady and her lover?" for I perceived that he was trotting off at full gallop in another direction, "how did they come on?"

"Oh, ay! As young folk generally do in such cases. From exchanging looks, they came to exchanging letters and then words. Stolen meetings and presents of hearts cut out of turnips, with a skewer put through them, to show the desperation of the case. That was the way at least that I went a courting my Martha, and it took amazingly."

"Hang you, and your Martha!" thought I, as I turned helplessly to the beef-steak, but I felt too much excited to do it the least justice. After deliberately knocking the ashes from his pipe, and taking a long draught of ale from the pewter-pot beside him, the old farmer went on of his own accord.

"I s'pose the young man told Miss Ellen that he could not live without her. We all tell 'em so, but we never dies a bit the sooner, for all that; and the pretty Miss told him to speak to her father, and he did speak, and to his surprise, old parson did not like it at all, and did not give him a very civil answer; and turned the young chap out of the house. He said that he did not approve of sporting characters for sons-in-law, and Miss Ellen should never get his consent to marry him. But as I told you before, sir, the women-folk will have their own way, especially when there is a sweet-heart or a new bonnet in the case; and the young lady gave him her own consent, and they took French leave and went off without saying a word to nobody. Next morning old parson was running about the village, asking everybody if they had seen his child, the tears running over his thin face, and he raving like a man out of his head."

"And were the young people ever married?" and in spite of myself I felt the colour flush my face to crimson.

"I never heard to the contrary. But it was not right to vex the poor old man: he took it so to heart, that it quite broke his spirit, and he lived but a very few months after she left him. His death was a great loss to the neighbourhood. We never had a parson that could hold a candle to him since. He was a father to the poor, and it was a thousand pities to see the good old man pining and drooping from day to day, and fretting himself after the spoilt gal who forsook him in his old age."

"You are too hard upon the young lady," said Suds: "it was but human nature after all, and small blame in her to prefer a young husband to an old snuffy superannuated parson."

"Did she ever return to ———?"

"She came to see her father in his dying illness, but too late to receive his forgiveness, for he died while her step was on the stairs. His last words —'Thank God, Ellen is come, I shall see her before I die.' But he did not, for he expired directly the words were out of his mouth. She and her husband followed the old man to his grave, and barring her grief, I never saw a handsomer couple."

"Do you know," said I, hesitatingly, "the church in which they were married?"

"I never heard, sir, not feeling curious to ask, as it did not concern me, but Mrs. Hepburn up at the Grove knows: she was Miss Lee then, and she and old parson's daughter went to school together, and were fast friends."

"Thank you," I replied carelessly, drawing my chair from the table, "you have satisfied my curiosity."

Though outwardly calm my heart was beating violently. Could it be true that I was in the immediate vicinity of Catherine and her aunt, and that the latter might be acquainted with the facts so important for me to procure?

The hopes and fears which this conversation had produced had the effect of destroying my appetite. It was in vain that the pretty widow tempted me with a number of delicacies in the shape of sweet home-made bread, delicious fresh butter, and humming ale, the power of mental excitement overpowered the mere gratification of the senses.

Before I retired for the night, I observed my loquacious companions doing ample justice to the savoury supper, from which I had risen with indifference.

I sought the solitude of my chamber, undressed, and flung myself into bed. To sleep was out of the question. Catherine Lee, Margaretta Moncton and my dear mother floated in a continual whirl through my heated brain. My mind was a perfect chaos of confused images and thoughts; nor could I reflect calmly on one subject for two minutes together. My head ached, my heart beat tumultuously, and in order to allay this feverish mental irritation, I took a large dose of laudanum, which produced the desired effect of lulling me into profound forgetfulness.

The day was far advanced when I shook off this heavy unwholesome slumber, but on endeavouring to rise, I felt so stupid and giddy, that I was fain to take a cup of coffee in bed. A table-spoonful of lime-juice administered by the white hand of Mrs. Archer, counteracted the unpleasant effects of the opiate.

CHAPTER VIII.
ELM GROVE.

On calmly reviewing the conversation of the past night, I determined to walk over to Elm Grove, and confide my situation to Mrs. Hepburn, who, as a friend of my mother's, might feel more interested in me, than she had done in Mr. Robert Moncton's poor dependent clerk.

I was so well pleased with this plan that I immediately put it into execution, and gave myself no time to alter my resolution, until I found myself waiting the appearance of the lady in an elegant drawing-room, which commanded the most beautiful prospect of hill and dale, in that most beautiful and romantic of English counties.

Mrs. Hepburn was past the meridian of life. Her countenance was by no means handsome, but the expression was gentle and agreeable, and her whole appearance lady-like and prepossessing. She had mingled a great deal in the world, which had given her such a perfect control over her features, that little could be read of the inward emotions of the mind, from the calm and almost immovable placidity of her face.

A slight look of surprise at the sight of a visitor so unexpected, and in all probability equally unwelcome, made me feel most keenly the awkwardness of the situation in which I was placed. The cold and courteous manner in which she asked to what cause she was indebted for the pleasure of a visit from Mr. Geoffrey Moncton, did not tend to diminish my confusion. I suffered my agitation so completely to master me, that for a few seconds I could find no words wherewith to frame the most common-place answer.

Observing my distress, she begged me to take a seat, and placing herself on the opposite side of the table, she continued to regard me with the most provoking *nonchalance*.

Making a desperate effort to break the oppressive silence, I contrived at last to stammer out, "I hope, madam, you will excuse the liberty I have taken by thus intruding myself upon your notice; but business of a very delicate and distressing nature induced me to apply to you, as the only person at all likely to befriend me in my present difficulty."

Her look of surprise increased; nor do I wonder at it, considering the ambiguity of my speech. What must she have thought? Nothing very favourable to me, I am sure. I could have bitten my tongue off for my want of tact, but the blunder was out, and she answered with some asperity:—"That we were almost strangers to each other, and that she could not imagine in what way she could serve me, without my request was a pecuniary one, in which case she owed me a debt of gratitude which she would gladly repay; that she had heard with sorrow from Mr. Theophilus Moncton, the manner in which I had been expelled from his father's office; that she bitterly lamented she or her niece should have directly or indirectly been the cause of my disgrace. She had been told, however, that the cause of Mr. Moncton's displeasure originated in my own rash conduct, and she feared that no application from her in my behalf, would be likely to effect a reconciliation between me and my uncle."

The colour burnt upon my cheek, and I answered with some warmth: "God forbid! that I should ever seek it at his hands! It is neither to solicit charity nor to complain to you, Mrs. Hepburn, of my past ill-treatment, that I sought an interview with you this morning. But—but"—and my voice faltered, and my eyes sought the ground, "I was told last night that you were the intimate friend of my mother."

"And who, sir, was your mother?"

"Her name was Ellen Rivers."

"Good Heavens! you the son of Ellen Rivers!" and the calm face became intensely agitated. "You, Geoffrey Moncton, the child of my first and dearest friend! I was told you were the natural son of her husband."

"But was he her husband?" and I almost gasped for breath.

"Who dares to doubt it?"

"This same honourable uncle of mine. He positively affirms that my mother was never lawfully the wife of Edward Moncton. He has branded the names of my parents with infamy, and destroyed every document which could prove my legitimacy. The only advantage which I derived from a niggardly destiny, my good name, has been wrenched from me by this cold-blooded villain!"

I was too much excited to speak with moderation; I trembled with passion.

"Be calm, Mr. Geoffrey," said Mrs. Hepburn, speaking in a natural and affectionate tone. "Let us go at length into the matter, and if I can in any way assist you, I will do so most cheerfully; although I must confess, that as matters stand between the families just now, it is rather an awkward piece of business. Your uncle, perhaps, never knew that I was acquainted with Miss Rivers, or felt any interest in her fate. These deep-seeing men often overreach themselves. But let me hear the tale you have to tell, and then I can better judge of its truth or falsehood."

Encouraged by the change in Mrs. Hepburn's tone and bearing, I gave her a brief statement of the events of my life, up to the hour in which I came to an open rupture with my uncle; and he basely destroyed my articles, and I found myself cast upon the world without the means of subsistence.

Mrs. Hepburn was greatly astonished at the narration, and often interrupted me to express her indignation.

"And this is the man, who bears such a fair character to the world. The friend of the friendless, and the guardian of innocence! Geoffrey Moncton, you make me afraid of the world, of myself—of every one. But what are you doing for a living, and what brings you into Derbyshire?"

"I am living at present in the family of Sir Alexander Moncton, who has behaved in the most generous manner to his *poor relation*."

"You have in him a powerful protector."

"Yes, and I may add, without boasting, a sincere friend. It is at his expense, and on his instigation that I am here, in order to find out some clue by which I may trace the marriage of my dear mother, and establish a legitimate claim to the title and estates of Moncton, at the worthy Baronet's demise, an event, which may God keep far distant," I added with fervour. "If I fail in this object, the property devolves to Robert Moncton and his son."

"I see it, I see it all; but I fear, Mr. Geoffrey, that your uncle has laid his plans too deeply for us to frustrate. I feel no doubts, as to your mother's marriage, though I was not present when that event took place, but I can tell you the church in which the ceremony was performed. Your mother was just of age, and the consent of parents was unnecessary, as far as the legality of the marriage was concerned."

"God bless you!" cried I, taking the hand she extended to me, and pressing it heartily between my own. "My mother's son blesses you, for the kind sympathy you have expressed in his welfare. You are my good angel, and have inspired me with a thousand new and pleasing hopes."

"These will not, however, prove your legitimacy, my young friend," said she, with a smile, "so restrain your ardour for a more fortunate time. I have a letter from your mother, written the morning after her marriage, describing her feelings during the ceremony and the remorse which marred her happiness, for having disobeyed and abandoned her aged father. She mentions her old nurse, and her father's gardener, as being the only witnesses present, and remarks on the sexton giving her away, as a bad omen, that she felt superstitious about it, and that her husband laughed at her fears.

"The register of the marriage, you say, has been destroyed. The parties who witnessed it, are most likely gathered to their fathers. But the very circumstance of the register having been destroyed, and this letter of your mother's, will, I think, be greatly in your favour. At all events, the parish of —— is only a pleasant ride among the Derby hills; and you can examine the registers for a trifling donation to the clerk; and ascertain from him, whether Mr. Roche, the clergyman who then resided in the parish, or his sexton, are still living. I will now introduce you to my niece, who always speaks of you with interest, and refuses to believe the many things advanced by your cousin to your disadvantage."

"Just like Miss Lee," said I. "She is not one to listen to the slanders of an enemy, behind one's back. I heard in the village, that Mr. Theophilus was in this neighbourhood, and a suitor of Miss Lee's."

"A mere village gossip. He is staying with Mr. Thurton, who lives in the pretty old-fashioned house, you passed on the hill on your way hither, and is a frequent visitor here. Mr. Moncton is anxious to promote an alliance between his son and my niece. In birth and fortune they are equals, and the match, in a worldly point of view, unexceptional."

"And Theophilus?"

"Is the most devoted of lovers."

"Execrable villain! and his poor young wife dying at the Hall of a broken heart. Can such things be, and the vengeance of heaven sleep!"

"You don't mean to insinuate that Mr. Theophilus Moncton is a married man."

"I scorn insinuations, I speak of facts; which to his face, I dare him to deny."

"My dear Kate!" cried Mrs. Hepburn sinking back in her chair. "I have combated for several weeks with what I considered an unreasonable prejudice on her part against this marriage. And this very morning I was congratulating myself on the possibility of getting her to receive Mr. Moncton's suit more favourably. Ah, Mr. Geoffrey! doubly her preserver, your timely visit has saved the dear girl from unutterable misery."

I then informed Mrs. Hepburn of all the particulars of this unfortunate marriage. Of young Moncton's desertion and barbarous treatment of his wife —of her attempted suicide, and the providential manner in which she had been rescued by me from the grave.

This painful interview, which had lasted several hours, was at length terminated by the entrance of Miss Lee and Theophilus, who had been absent riding with some friends.

They entered from the garden, and Mrs. Hepburn and I were so deeply engaged in conversation that we did not notice their approach until Catherine called out in a tone of alarm:—"Mr. Geoffrey Moncton here, and my aunt in tears? What can have happened?"

"Yes, Kate, you will be glad to see an old friend," said her aunt. "To you, Mr. Moncton," turning to Theophilus, "he is the bearer of sad tidings."

"Anything happened to my father?" said Theophilus, looking towards me with an expression in his green eyes, of intense and hungry inquiry, which for a moment overcame his first glance of aversion and contempt.

I read the meaning of that look, and answered scorn for scorn.

"Of your father and *his* affairs I know nothing. The tie of kindred is broken between us. I wish that I knew as little of you and yours."

"What do you mean?" and his pale cheek flushed with crimson. "Is it to traduce my character, to insult me before ladies, that you dare to intrude yourself in my company? What brings you here? What message have you for me?"

"With you," I said, coldly, "I have no business, nor did I ever wish to see you again. My steps were guided here by that Providence which watches over the innocent, and avenges the wrongs of the injured. It is not my nature to stab even an enemy in the dark. What I have to say to you will be said openly and to your face."

"This is fine language," said he, bursting into a scornful laugh. "On what provincial theatre have you been studying, since you were expelled my father's office?"

"I have not yet learned to act the part of the hypocrite and betrayer, in the great drama of life; or by lying and deceit to exalt myself upon the ruin of others."

"Go on, go on," cried he, "I perceive your drift. You are a better actor than you imagine yourself. Such accusations as you can bring against me, will redound more to my credit than praise from such lips."

"Theophilus Moncton," I replied, calmly, "I did not invade the sanctity of this roof in order to meet and quarrel with you. What I have to say to you I will communicate elsewhere."

"Here, sir, if you please—here to my face. I am no coward, and that you know of old. I am certain that you cannot name anything to my disadvantage, but what I am able triumphantly to refute."

"Well—be it so then. I find you here a suitor for this lady's hand. Four days ago your wife attempted suicide, and was rescued from a watery grave by my arm."

"Liar! 'tis false! Do not listen, ladies, to this vile calumniator. He has a purpose of his own to serve, by traducing my character to my friends. Let him bring witnesses more worthy of credit than himself, before you condemn me."

"I condemn no one, Mr. Theophilus," said Mrs. Hepburn, gravely. "Sir Alexander Moncton is a person of credit, and your wife is at present under his protection. What can you say to this?"

She spoke in vain. Theophilus left the room without deigning to reply. We looked in silence at each other.

Miss Lee was the first who spoke:—"He is convicted by his own conscience. I thought him cold and selfish, but never dreamed that he was a villain. And the poor young woman, his wife, what is her name?"

"Alice Mornington."

A faint cry burst from the lips of Catherine. I caught her in my arms before she fell, and placed her in a chair: she had fainted. Mrs. Hepburn rang the bell for one of her female attendants, and amid the bustle and confusion of removing Miss Lee to her own apartment, I took the opportunity of retiring from the scene.

"What new mystery does this involve?" said I, half aloud, as I sauntered down the thick avenue which led from the house to the high-road. "Why did the mention of that name produce such an effect upon Catherine? She cannot be acquainted with the parties. Her agitation might be accidental. 'Tis strange —very strange"——

"Stop!" cried a loud voice near me; and pale and haggard, his hands fiercely clenched, and his eyes starting from his head, Theophilus confronted me.

"Geoffrey, this meeting must be our last."

"With all my heart;" and folding my arms I looked him steadfastly in the face.

Never shall I forget the expression of that countenance, transformed as it was with furious passion; livid, convulsed; every feature swollen and quivering with malice and despair. It was dreadful to contemplate—scarcely human.

How often since has it haunted me in dreams.

The desire of revenge had overcome his usual caution. In the mood he was then in, his puny figure would have been a match for a giant.

"I seek no explanation of your conduct," said he: "we hate each other;" he gnashed his teeth as he spoke. "I have ruined you, and you have done your best to return the compliment. But you shall not triumph in my disgrace: if we fall it shall be together."

He sprang upon me unawares. He wound his thin sinewy arms around me. I was taken by surprise, and before I could raise my arm to defend myself from his ferocious attack, I was thrown heavily to the ground. The last thing that I can distinctly recollect was his thin bony fingers grasping my throat.

CHAPTER IX.
MY NURSE, AND WHO SHE WAS.

The night was far advanced when I recovered my senses. The room I occupied was large and spacious; the bed on which I was lying such as wealth supplies to her most luxurious children. One watch-light with shaded rays, scarcely illuminated a small portion of the ample chamber, leaving the remote corners in intense shade. A female figure, in a long, loose, white wrapping-gown, was seated at the table reading. Her back was towards me, and my head was too heavy and my eyes too dim to recognize the person of the stranger.

I strove to lift my head from the pillow; the effort wrung from my lips a moan of pain. This brought the lady instantly to my side. It was Mrs. Hepburn's face, but it faded from my sight like the faces that look upon us in dreams. Recollection and sight failed me—I remember nothing more.

Many days passed unconsciously over me. Nearly three weeks elapsed before I was able to bear the light, or ask an explanation of the past.

Mrs. Hepburn and Miss Lee were my constant attendants, and a middle-aged, respectable man in livery, who slept in my apartment, and rendered me the most kind and essential services. Dan Simpson was an old servant of the family; had been born on the estate, and lived for thirty years under that roof. He was a worthy, pious man, and during my long, tedious illness we contracted a mutual friendship which lasted to the close of his life. Had it not been for the care and attention of those excellent women and honest Dan, I might never have lived to be the chronicler of these adventures.

As I recovered strength, Simpson informed me that the gamekeeper had witnessed from behind the hedge my encounter with Theophilus, and prevented further mischief by bursting suddenly upon my adversary, who had the dastardly meanness to give me several blows after I was insensible.

Theophilus left his victim with savage reluctance. The gamekeeper thought at first that I was dead, and he told him that he had better be off, or he would inform against him, and have him convicted for murder. This hint was enough, and Theophilus lost no time in quitting the neighbourhood.

I had fallen with the back of my head against the trunk of a large elm tree, which had caused concussion of the brain.

"You must be quite still, sir, and talk as little as possible, or 'twill be bad for you," said Simpson. "An' the ladies must come near you as seldom as they can. We may manage to keep you silent, sir, but I'll be dashed, if it be possible to keep women's tongues from wagging. They will talk—no matter the danger to themselves or others; an' 'tis 'most impossible for a man not to listen to them. They be so good and pretty. I'd advise you, Master Geoffrey, to shut your eyes, when our young lady comes in with the mistress to see you, an' then you'll no be tempted to open your ears."

There was a good deal of wholesome truth in honest Dan's advice, but I lacked the resolution to adopt it. My eyes and ears were always wide open when my fair nurse and her aunt approached my bed-side.

It was delightful to me, to listen to the soft tones of Kate Lee's musical voice, when her sweet fair face was bending over me, and she inquired in such an earnest and tender manner, "how I was, and how I had passed the night."

"Always the better for seeing and hearing you, charming Kate," I would have answered had I dared.

One afternoon, Kate was absent, and the dear old lady, her good aunt came to sit with me, and read to me while she was away. It was always good pious books she read, and I tried to feel interested; but they were dull, and never failed in putting me to sleep. Knowing the result, I always listened patiently, and in less than half an hour was certain to obtain my reward.

I have no doubt, that the soporific quality of these sermons, by quieting my mind and producing wholesome repose, did more to advance my recovery, than all the lotions and medicines administered by the family physician, who was another worthy but exceedingly prosy individual.

It so happened that this afternoon my kind old friend was inclined for a chat. She sat down near my bed, and after feeling my pulse, and telling me that I was going on nicely, she began to talk over my late misadventure.

"It is a mercy that your life was spared, Geoffrey. Who could have imagined that your cousin, with his smooth courteous manners and silken voice was such a ruffian."

"The snake is beautiful and graceful," said I, "yet the venom it conceals produces death. Theophilus has many qualities in common with the reptile. Smooth, insidious, and deadly; he always strikes to kill."

"His encounter with you, Geoffrey, has removed every doubt from our minds, as to his real character and the truth of your statements. I cannot think, without a shudder, of the bare possibility of my amiable Kate becoming the wife of such a villain."

"Could Miss Lee really entertain the least regard for such a man?" cried I, indignant at the bare supposition.

"Hush! Geoffrey. You must not talk above a whisper. You know Dr. Lake has forbidden you to do that. Kate never loved Theophilus. She might, however, have yielded to my earnest importunities for her to become his wife. Mr. Moncton is her guardian, and some difficulties attend the settlement of her property, which this union would in all probability have removed. You know the manner in which some lawyers cut out work for themselves, Mr. Moncton. I have no doubt, it is the only real obstacle in the way."

"More than probable," whispered I, for I wanted the old lady to go on talking about Kate; "but, dear Mrs. Hepburn, I have a perfect horror of these marriages without affection; they seldom turn out well. Poor as I am I would never sacrifice the happiness of a whole life by contracting such a marriage."

"Young people always think so, but a few years produce a great change in their sentiments. I am always sorry when I hear of a young man or woman being desperately in love, for it generally ends in disappointment. A heavy trial of this kind—a most unfortunate engagement in early youth, has rendered poor Catherine indifferent to the voice of love."

I felt humbled and mortified by this speech. I turned upon my pillow to conceal my face from my kind nurse. Good heavens! Could it be true, that I had only loved the phantom of a dream—had followed for so many weary months a creature of imagination—a woman who had no heart to bestow upon her humble worshipper?

I had flattered myself that I was not indifferent to Miss Lee: had even dared to hope that she loved me. What visions of future happiness in store for me, had these presumptuous hopes foretold. What stately castles had I not erected upon this sandy foundation, which I was now doomed to see perish, as it were within my grasp?

My bosom heaved, and my eyes became dim, but I proudly struggled with my feelings, and turning to Mrs. Hepburn, I inquired with apparent calmness, "If any letters had arrived for me?" She said she did not know, but would send to the post-office and inquire.

I then, by mere chance, remembered the name Sir Alexander had bestowed upon me, and told Simpson, who had just then entered, to ask for letters for Mr. Tremain.

I felt restless and unhappy, and feigned sleep, in order to be left alone; and when alone, if a few tears did come to my relief, to cool the fever in my heart and brain, the reader who has ever loved will excuse the weakness.

I could not forgive my charming Kate, for having loved another, when I felt that she ought to have loved me. Had I not saved her life at the risk of my own? had I not been true to her at the sacrifice of my best interests, and slighted the pure devoted affection of Margaretta Moncton, for the love of one who loved me not—who never had loved me, though I had worshipped her image in the innermost shrine of my heart? Alas! for poor human nature: this severe trial was more than my philosophy could bear.

From these painful and mortifying reflections, I was aroused by the light step of the beautiful delinquent, who, radiant in youth and loveliness, entered the room. I glanced at her from under my half-closed eyelids. I regarded her as a fallen angel. She had dared to love another, and half her beauty had vanished.

She came to my bed-side, and in accents of the tenderest concern, inquired after my health.

"What have you been doing, Geoffrey: not talking too much, I hope? You look ill and feverish. See, I have brought you a present—a nosegay of wild flowers, gathered in the woods. Are they not beautiful?"

To look into her sweet face, and entertain other feelings than those of respect and admiration, was impossible. I took the flowers from the delicate white hand that proffered them, and tried to thank her. My lips quivered. I sighed involuntarily, and turned away.

"You are out of spirits, Geoffrey, my dear friend," said she, sitting down by my bed-side, and placing her finger on the pulse of the emaciated hand which lay listlessly on the coverlid: "you must try and overcome these fits of depression, or you will never get well. I left you cheerful and hopeful. My dear aunt has been preaching one of her long sermons, I fear, and that has made you nervous and melancholy."

Another deep sigh and a shake of the head—I could neither look at her, nor trust myself to speak.

"Your long confinement in this dull room affects your mind, Geoffrey. It is hard to be debarred the glorious air of heaven during such lovely summer weather. But cheer up, brave heart, in a few days, the doctor says, that you may be removed into another room. From the windows you will then enjoy a delightful prospect, and watch the sun set every evening behind the purple hills."

"You and your kind aunt are too good to me, Miss Lee. To one in my unfortunate circumstances, it would have been better for me had I died."

"For shame! Geoffrey. Such sentiments are unworthy of you—are ungrateful to the merciful Father who saved you from destruction."

"Why, what inducements have I to live?"

"Many; if it be only to improve the talents which God has committed to your keeping. For this end your life has been spared, and the heavier will be your amount of guilt, if you neglect so great salvation. God has permitted you to assert your innocence—to triumph over your enemy; has saved you from the premeditated malice of that enemy; and do you feel no gratitude to Him for such signal mercies?"

"Indeed I have not thought of my preservation in this way before, nor have I been so grateful as I ought to have been. I have suffered human passions and affections to stand between me and heaven."

"We are all too prone to do that, Geoffrey. The mind, in its natural and unconverted state, cannot comprehend the tender mercies of the Creator. Human nature is so selfish, when left to its own guidance, that it needs the purifying influences of religion to lift the soul from grovelling in the dust. I am no bigot—no disputer about creeds and forms of worship, but I know that without God no one can be happy or contented in any station of life, under any circumstances."

Seeing that I did not answer, she released the hand that she had retained within her own, and said very gently:

"Forgive me, Geoffrey, if I have wounded your feelings."

"Go on—go on. I could hear you talk for ever, dear Miss Lee."

"You have grown very formal; Geoffrey—why Miss Lee? During your illness, I have been simple Kate."

"But I am getting well now," and I tried to smile; my heart was too sore. "Oh, Catherine," I cried, "forgive my waywardness, for I am very unhappy."

"You have been placed in very trying circumstances, but I feel an inward conviction that you will overcome them all."

"My grief, has nothing to do with that," said I, looking at her very earnestly.

I read in her countenance pity and surprise, but no tenderer emotion.

"May I—dare I, dearest Catherine, unburden my heart to you?"

"Speak freely and candidly, Geoffrey. If I cannot remove the cause of your distress, you maybe certain of my advice and sympathy."

"Heaven bless you for that!" I murmured, kissing the hand which disengaged itself gently from my grasp, and with a colour somewhat heightened, Catherine bent towards me in a listening attitude.

The ice once broken, I determined to tell her all; and in low and broken accents I proceeded to inform her of my boyish attachment, and the fond hopes I had dared to entertain, from the kind and flattering manner in which she had returned my attentions at Mr. Moncton's, and of the utter annihilation of these ardently cherished hopes, when informed by Mrs. Hepburn that afternoon, that her affections had been bestowed upon some more fortunate person.

During my incoherent confession, Miss Lee was greatly agitated. Her face was turned from me, but from the listless attitude of her figure, and the motionless repose of the white hand which fell over the arm of the chair in which she was seated, I saw that she was weeping.

Then came a long, painful pause. Catherine at length wiped away her tears, and broke the oppressive silence.

"Geoffrey," said she, solemnly, "I have been to blame in this. At the time you saved my life (a service for which I can never feel sufficiently grateful, for I value life and all its mercies) I was young and happy, engaged to one, who in many respects, though older by some years, resembled yourself.

"When I met you the second time at your uncle's, disappointment had flung a baleful shade over my first fond anticipations of life; but, young and sanguine, I still hoped for the best. By some strange coincidence, your voice and manner greatly resembled those of the man I loved, and whom I still fondly hoped to meet again. This circumstance attracted me towards you, and I felt great pleasure in conversing with you, as every look and tone reminded me of him. This, doubtless, gave rise to the attachment you have just revealed to me, and which I must unceasingly lament, as it is impossible for me to make you any adequate return."

"And is my rival still dear to you, Miss Lee?"

Her lips again quivered, and she turned weeping away.

"I read my fate in your silence. You love him yet?"

"And shall continue to love him whilst I have life, Geoffrey Moncton," slowly and suffocatingly broke from the pale lips of the trembling girl.

"And you would have been persuaded by your aunt to marry Theophilus Moncton."

"Never! Who told you that?" and her eye flashed proudly, almost scornfully upon me.

"Your good aunt."

"She knows nothing about it. I ceased to oppose her wishes in words, because I found that it might produce a rupture between us. Women of my aunt's age have outlived their sympathies in affairs of the heart. What they once felt they have forgotten, or look upon as a weakness which ought not to be tolerated in their conversations with the young. But look at that fine, candid face, Geoffrey; that open benevolent brow, and tell me, if having once loved the original, it is such an easy matter to forget or to find a substitute in such a being as Theophilus Moncton."

As she said this she took a portrait that was suspended by a gold chain from the inner folds which covered her beautiful bosom, and placed it in my hand.

"Good heavens!" cried I, sinking back upon the pillow, "my friend, *George Harrison*!"

"Who? I know no one of that name."

"True—true. George Harrison—Philip Mornington—they are the same. And his adored and lost Charlotte Laurie, and my beautiful Catherine Lee are identified. I see through it now. He hid the truth from me, fearing that it might destroy our friendship. Honesty in this, as in all other cases, would have been the best policy."

"Philip is still alive! Not hearing of him for so many months made me conclude that he was either dead or had left England in disgust."

"He still lives, and loves you, Kate, with all the fervour of a first attachment."

"I do not deserve it, Geoffrey. I dared to mistrust his honour, to base listen to calumnies propagated by Theophilus and his father, purposely, I now believe, to injure him in my estimation. But what young girl, ignorant of the world and the ways of designing men, could suspect such a grave, plausible man as Robert Moncton, who outwardly always manifested the most affectionate interest in my happiness? I much fear that my coldness had a very bad effect upon Philip's character, and was the means of leading him into excesses, which ultimately led to his ruin."

I was perplexed, and knew not what answer to make, for she had hit upon the plain truth. To tell her so, was to plunge an amiable creature into the deepest affliction, and to withhold it was not doing justice to the friend, whom, above all men I valued.

With the quick eye of love, and the tact of woman, Kate perceived my confusion, and guessed the cause; she broke into a fit of passionate weeping.

"Dear Kate," I began, with difficulty raising myself on the pillow, "control this violent emotion, and I will tell you all I know of my friend."

She looked eagerly up through her tears; but the task I had imposed upon myself was beyond my strength to fulfil. My nerves were so completely shattered by the agitating effects of the past scene, that I sank back exhausted and gasping on the pillow.

"Not now, not now, Geoffrey, you are unequal to the task. This conversation has tried you too much." And raising my head upon her arm, she bathed my temples with eau de Cologne, and hastened to administer a restorative from the phial that stood on the table.

"I shall be better now I know the worst," said I; and closing my eyes for a few moments, my head rested passively on her snow-white shoulder.

A few hours back, and the touch of those fair hands would have thrilled my whole frame with delight; but now it awoke in me little or no emotion. The beautiful dream had vanished. My adored Catherine Lee was the betrothed of my friend; and I could gaze upon her pale agitated face with calmness—with brotherly, platonic love. I was only now anxious to effect a reconciliation between George and his Kate, I rejoiced that the means were in all probability in my power.

The entrance of Mrs. Hepburn with letters, put an end to this painful scene; while their contents gave rise to other thoughts and feelings, hopes and fears.

"I cannot read them yet," said I, after having examined the handwriting in which the letters were directed. "My eyes are dim. I am too weak. The rest of an hour will restore me. The sight of these letters makes me nervous, and agitates me too much. They are from Sir Alexander and his daughter, and may contain important tidings."

"Let us go, dear aunt," whispered Kate, slipping her arm through Mrs. Hepburn's. "It will be better to leave Geoffrey for awhile alone."

They left the room instantly. I was relieved by their absence. My heart was oppressed with painful thoughts. I wanted to be alone—to commune with my own spirit, and be still.

A few minutes had scarcely elapsed, before I was sound asleep.

CHAPTER X.
MY LETTERS.

Day was waning into night, when I again unclosed my eyes. A sober calm had succeeded the burning agitation of the previous hours. I was no longer a lover—or at least the lover of Catherine Lee. My thoughts had returned to Moncton Park, and in dreams the fairy figure of Margaret had flitted beside me, through its green arcades. My heart was free to love her who so loved me, and by the light of the lamp I eagerly opened up the letters, which I had grasped during my slumbers tightly in my hand.

But before I could decipher a line, my worthy friend Dan came to the rescue. "I cannot permit that, Master Geoffrey," said he; "your eyes are too weak to read such fine penmanship."

"My good fellow, only a few lines. You must allow me to do that."

"Not a word. What is the use of all this nursing if you will have your own way? You will be dead at this rate in less than a week."

"What a deal of trouble that would save you!" said I, looking at him reproachfully.

"Who called it trouble? not I," said honest Dan. "The trouble is a pleasure, if you will only be tractable and obey those who mean you well. Now don't you see what comes of acting against reason and common sense. You would talk to the mistress the whole blessed afternoon. Several times I came to the door, and it was still talk, talk, talk; and when my young lady comes home and the old mistress was fairly tired, and walked out to give her tongue a rest, it was still the same with the young one—talk, talk, talk, and no end to the talk, till you well nigh fainted; and if it had not been for God's Providence that set you off fast asleep, you might have died of the talk fever."

"But I am better now, Daniel: you see the talking did me no harm, but good."

"Tout! tout! man, a bad excuse, you know, is better than none they say. But I think it's far worse, for 'tis generally an invented lie, just to cheat the Devil or one's own conscience; howsomever, I doubt much whether the Devil was ever cheated by such practices, but did not always win in the long run by that sort of *stale mate*."

"Are you a chess player?" I asked in some surprise.

"Ay, just in a small way. Old Jenkins the butler and I often have a tuzzle together in his pantry, which sometimes ends in a *stale mate*—he! he! he!—Jenkins, who is a dry stick, says that a stale mate is better than stale fish, or a glass of flat champagne—he! he! he!"

"I perfectly agree with Jenkins. But don't you see, my good Daniel, that you blame me for talking with the ladies, and wanting to read a love-letter; while you are making me act quite as imprudently, by laughing and talking with you."

"A love-letter did you say?" and he poked his long nose nearly into my face, and squinted down with a glance of intense curiosity at the open letter I still held in my hand. "Why that is rather a temptation to a young gentleman, I must own; cannot I read it for you, sir? I am as good a scholar as our clerk."

"I don't at all doubt your capabilities, Simpson. But you see, this is a thing I really can only do for myself. The young lady would not like her letter to be made public."

"Why, Lord, sir, you don't imagine that I would say a word about it. I have kept secrets before now; ay, and ladies' secrets too. I was the man who helped your father to carry off Miss Ellen. It was I held the horses at the corner of the lane, while he took her out of the chamber-window. I drove them to—— church next morning, and waited at the doors till they were married; and your poor father gave me five golden guineas to drink the bride's health. Ah! she was a bride worth the winning. A prettier woman I never saw: she beat my young lady hollow, though some folks do think Miss Catherine a beauty."

"You did not witness the ceremony?"

"No, sir; but as I sat on the box of the carriage, I saw old Parson Roche go up to the aisle in his white gown, with a book in his hand, and if it were not to marry the young folks, what business had he there?"

"What, indeed!" thought I. "This man's evidence may be of great value to me."

I lay silent for some minutes thinking over these circumstances, and quite forgot my letter until reminded of it by Simpson.

"Well, sir, I'm thinking that I will allow you to read that letter; if you will just put on my spectacles to protect your eyes from the light."

"But I could not see with them, Simpson; spectacles, like wives, seldom suit anybody but the persons to whom they belong. Besides, you know, old eyes and young eyes never behold the same objects alike."

"Maybe," said the old man. "But do just wait patiently until I can prop you up in the bed, and put the lamp near enough for you to see that small writing. Tzet, tzet—what a pity it is that young ladies, now-a-days, are ashamed of writing a good, legible hand. You will require a double pair of specs to read yon."

The old man's curiosity was almost as great as his kindness; and I should have felt annoyed at his peeping and prying over my shoulder, had I not been certain that he could not decipher, without the aid of the said spectacles, a single word of the contents. I was getting tired of his loquacity, and was at last obliged to request him to go, which he did most reluctantly, begging me as he left the room to have mercy on my poor eyes.

There was some need of the caution; for the fever had left me so weak that it was with great difficulty I succeeded in reading Margaretta's letter.

"Dear Cousin Geoffrey,

"We parted with an assurance of mutual friendship. I shall not waste words in apologizing for writing to you. As a friend I may continue to love and value you, convinced that the heart in which I trust will never condemn me for the confidence I repose in it.

"I have suffered a severe affliction since you left us, in the death of poor Alice, which took place a fortnight ago. She died in a very unsatisfactory frame of mind, anxious to the last to behold her unprincipled husband or Dinah North. The latter, however, has disappeared, and no trace of her can be discovered.

"There was some secret, perhaps the same that you endeavoured so fruitlessly to wrest from her, which lay heavily upon the poor girl's conscience, and which she appeared eager to communicate after the power of utterance had fled. The repeated mention of her brother's name during the day which preceded her dissolution, led me to the conclusion that whatever she had to divulge was connected with him. But she is gone, and the secret has perished with her, a circumstance which we may all have cause to regret.

"And this is the first time, Geoffrey, that I have looked upon death—the death of one, whom from infancy I have loved as a sister. The sight has filled me with awe and terror; the more so, because I feel a strange presentiment that my own end is not far distant.

"This, my dear cousin, you will say is the natural result of watching the decay of one so young and beautiful as Alice Mornington—one, who, a few brief months ago, was full of life, and health, and hope; that her death has brought more forcibly before me the prospect of my own mortality. Perhaps it is so. I do not wish to die, Geoffrey; life, for me, has many charms. I love my dear father tenderly. To his fond eyes I am the light of life— the sole thing which remains to him of my mother. I would live for his sake to cherish and comfort him in his old age. I love the dear old homestead with all its domestic associations, and I could not bid adieu to you, my dear cousin, without keen regret.

"And then, the glorious face of nature—the fields, the flowers, the glad, bright sunbeams, the rejoicing song of birds, the voice of waters, the whispered melodies of wind-stirred leaves, the green solitudes of the dim mysterious forest, I love—oh, how I love them all!

"Yes, these are dear to my heart and memory; yet I wander discontentedly amid my favourite haunts. My eyes are ever turned to the earth. A spirit seems to whisper to me in low tones, 'Open thy arms, mother, to receive thy child.'

"I struggle with these waking phantasies; my eyes are full of tears. I feel the want of companionship. I long for some friendly bosom to share my grief and wipe away my tears. The sunshine of my heart has vanished. Ah, my dear friend, how earnestly I long for your return! Do write, and let us know how you have sped. My father came back to the Hall the day after the funeral of poor Alice. He marvels like me at your long silence. He has important news to communicate which I must not forestall.

"Write soon, and let us know that you are well and happy; a line from you will cheer my drooping heart.

"Yours, in the sincerity of love,

"Margaretta Moncton.

"Moncton Park, July 22, 18—."

I read this letter over several times, until the characters became misty, and I could no longer form them into words. A thousand times I pressed it to my lips, and vowed eternal fidelity to that dear writer. Yet what a mournful tale it told! The love but half-concealed, was apparent in every line. I felt bitterly, that I was the cause of her dejection; that hopeless affection for me was undermining her health.

I would write to her instantly—would tell her all. Alas! my hand, unnerved by long illness, could no longer guide the pen—and how could I employ the hand of another? I cursed my unlucky accident, and the unworthy cause of it: and in order to divert my thoughts from this melancholy subject, I eagerly tore open Sir Alexander's letter.

The paper fell from my grasp, I was not able to read.

Mrs. Hepburn appeared like a good angel, followed by honest Dan, bearing candles, and the most refreshing of all viands to an invalid—a delicious cup of fragrant tea, the very smell of which was reviving; and whilst deliberately sipping the contents of my second cup, I requested Mrs. Hepburn, as a great favour, to read to me Sir Alexander's letter.

"Perhaps it may contain family secrets?" said she, with an inquiring look, whilst her hand rested rather tenaciously upon the closely written sheets.

"After the confidence which we have mutually reposed in each other, my dear madam, I can have no secret to conceal. You are acquainted with my private history, and I flatter myself, that neither you, nor your amiable niece, are indifferent to my future welfare."

"You only do us justice, Geoffrey," said the kind woman, affectionately pressing my hand, after re-adjusting my pillows. "I love you for your mother's sake; I prize you for your own; and I hope you will allow me to consider you in the light of that son, of whom Heaven early deprived me."

"You make a rich man of me at once," I cried, respectfully kissing her hand. "How can I be poor—while I possess so many excellent friends? Robert Moncton, with all his wealth, is a beggar, when compared to the hitherto despised Geoffrey."

"Well, let us leave off complimenting each other," said Mrs. Hepburn, laughing; "and please to lie down like a good boy and compose yourself, and listen attentively to what your uncle has to say to you."

"MY DEAR GEOFF.

"What the deuce, man, has happened to you, that we have received no tidings from you? Have you and old Dinah eloped together on the back of a broomstick. The old hag's disappearance looks rather suspicious. Madge does little else than pine and fret for your return. I begin to feel quite jealous of you in that quarter.

"I have a long tale to tell you, and scarcely know where to begin. Next to taking doctor's stuff, I detest letter-writing; and were you not a great favourite, the pens, ink, and paper might go to the bottom of the river, before I would employ them to communicate a single thought.

"I had a very pleasant journey to London, which terminated in a very unpleasant visit to your *worthy* uncle. It was not without great repugnance that I condescended to enter his house, particularly when I reflected on the errand which took me there. He received me with one of his blandest smiles, and inquired after my health with such affectionate interest, that it would have led a stranger to imagine he really wished me well, instead of occupying a snug corner in the family vault.

"How I abhor this man's hypocrisy! Bad as he is, that is the very worst feature in his character. I cut all his compliments short, however, by informing him that the object of my visit was one of a very unpleasant nature, which required his immediate attention.

"He looked very cold and spiteful. 'I anticipate your business,' said he; 'Geoffrey Moncton, I am informed, has found an asylum with you, and I suppose you are anxious to effect a reconciliation between us. If such be the purport of your visit, Sir Alexander, your journey must prove in vain. I never will forgive that ungrateful young man, nor admit him again into my presence.'

"'You have injured him too deeply, Robert,' said I, calmly (for you know, Geoff, that it is of little use flying into a passion with your cold-blooded uncle: he is not generous enough to get insulted and show fight like another man) 'Geoffrey does not wish it,' I replied, 'and I should scorn to ask it in his name.'

"The man of law looked incredulous, but did not choose to venture a reply.

"'It is not of Geoffrey Moncton, the independent warm-hearted orphan, I wished to speak, who, thank God! has pluck enough to take his own part, and speak for himself—it is of one, who is a disgrace to his name and family. I mean your son, Theophilus.'

"'Really, Sir Alexander, you take a great deal of trouble about matters which do not concern you,' (he said this with a sarcastic sneer) 'my son is greatly indebted to you for such disinterested kindness.'

"His cool impudence provoked me beyond endurance: I felt a wicked pleasure in retaliation, which God forgive me! was far from a Christian spirit. But I despised the rascal too much at that moment to pity him.

"'My interference in this matter concerns me more nearly than you imagine, Mr. Moncton,' said I. 'Your son's unfortunate wife attempted suicide, but was prevented in the act of drowning herself by the nephew you have traduced and treated so basely.'

"'Damn her! why did he not let her drown! thundered forth your uncle.'

"'Because his heart was not hardened in villainy like your own. Your daughter-in-law now lies dying at my house, and I wish to transfer the responsibility from my hands into your own.'

"'It was your fault that they ever met,' cried he: 'your love of low society which threw them together. Theophilus was not a man to make such a fool of himself—such an infernal fool!'

"And then the torrent burst. The man became transformed into the demon. He stamped and raved—and tore his hair, and cursed with the most horrid and blasphemous oaths, the son who had followed so closely in his own steps. Such a scene I never before witnessed—such a spectacle of human depravity may it never be my lot to behold again. In the midst of his incoherent ravings, he actually threatened, as the consummation of his indignation against his son, to make you his heir.

"Such is the contradiction inherent in our fallen nature, that he would exalt the man he hates, to revenge himself upon the son who has given the death-blow to the selfish pride which has marked his crooked path through life.

"I left him in deep disgust. It made me think very humbly of myself. Faith, Geoff, when I look back on my own early career, I begin to think that we are a bad set; and without you and Madge raise the moral tone of the family character there is small chance of any of the other members finding their way to heaven.

"I spent a couple of quiet days with my old friend Onslow, and then commenced my journey home. At a small village about thirty miles from London, I was overtaken by such a violent storm of thunder and rain, that I had to put up at the only inn in the place for the night.

"In the passage I was accosted by an old man of pleasing demeanour, and with somewhat of a foreign aspect, who inquired if he had the honour of speaking to Sir Alexander Moncton? I said yes, but that he had the advantage of me, as I believed him to be a perfect stranger.

"He appeared embarrassed, and said, that he did not wonder at my forgetting him, as it was only in a subordinate situation I had ever seen him, and that was many years ago.

"I now looked hard at the man, and a conviction of often having seen him before flashed into my mind. It was an image connected with bygone years—years of folly and dissipation.

"'Surely you are not William Walters, who for such a long time was the friend and confidant of Robert Moncton.'

"'The same, at your service.'

"'Mr. Walters,' said I, turning on my heel, 'I have no wish to resume the acquaintance.'

"'You are right,' replied he, and was silent for a minute or so, then resumed, in a grave and humble tone; 'Sir Alexander, I trust we are both better men, or the experience and sorrows of years have been given to us in vain. I can truly say, that I have deeply repented of my former sinful life, and I trust that my repentance has been accepted by that God before whom we must both soon appear. Still, I cannot blame you, for wishing to have no further intercourse with one whom you only knew as an unprincipled man. But for the sake of a young man, who, if living, is a near connection of yours, I beg you to listen patiently to what I have to say.'

"'If your communication has reference to Geoffrey, the son of Edward Moncton, and nephew to Robert, I am entirely at your service.'

"'He is the man! I have left a comfortable home in the United States, and returned to England with the sole object in view, of settling a moral debt which has lain a long time painfully on my conscience. I was just on my way to Moncton Park to speak to you on this important subject.'

"My dear Geoff, you may imagine the feelings with which I heard this announcement. Had I been alone I should have snapped my fingers, whistled, shouted for joy—anything that would have diminished with safety the suffocating feeling at my heart. I was so glad—I never knew how dear you were to me until then. So I invited the solemn, and rather puritanical-looking white-headed man to partake of my dinner, and spend the evening in my apartment, in order to get out of him all that I could concerning you. The result was most satisfactory. There was no need of bribes or nut-crackers; he was anxious to make a clean breast of it, for which I gave him ample absolution.

"Here is his confession, as well as I can remember it:—

"'My acquaintance with Robert Moncton commenced at school. I was the only son of a rich banker in the city of Norwich. My father was generous to a fault, and allowed me more pocket-money than my young companions could boast of receiving from their friends at home. My father had risen, by a train of fortunate circumstances, from a very humble station in life, and was ostentatiously proud of his wealth. He was particularly anxious for me to pass for the son of a very rich man at school, which he fancied would secure for me powerful friends, and their interest in my journey through life.

"'I was not at all averse to his plans, which I carried out to their fullest extent, and went by the name of *Ready-Money Jack*, among my school-mates, who I have no doubt whispered behind my back, that—fools and their money are soon parted; for you know, Sir Alexander, this is the way of the world. And there is no place in which the world and its selfish maxims are more fully exemplified than in a large boarding-school.

"'I had not been long at school when the two Monctons were admitted to the same class with myself. Edward was a dashing, eloquent, brave lad; more remarkable for a fine appearance and an admirable temper, than for any particular talent. He was a very popular boy, but somehow or other we did not take to each other.

"'The boyish vanity fostered by my father, made me wish to be considered the first lad in the school; a notion which Edward took good care to keep down; and fretted and galled by his assumption of superiority, I turned to Robert, who was everything but friendly to Edward, to support my cause and back me in my quarrels.

"'Robert was a handsome, gentlemanly-looking lad, but quite the reverse of Edward. He hated rough play, learned his lessons with indefatigable industry, and took good care to keep himself out of harm's way. He was the pattern boy of the school. The favourite of all the teachers. He possessed a grave, specious manner—a cold quiet reserve, which imposed upon the ignorant and unsuspecting; and his love of money was a passion which drew all the blood from his stern proud heart. He saw that I was frank and vain, and he determined to profit by my weakness. I did not want for natural capacity, but I was a sad idler.

"'Robert was shrewd and persevering, and I paid him handsomely for doing my sums and writing my Latin exercises. We became firm friends, and I loved him for years with more sincerity than he deserved.

"'As I advanced towards manhood, my poor father met with great losses; and on the failure of a large firm with which his own was principally connected, he became a bankrupt.

"'Solely dependent upon my rich father, without any fixed aim or object in life, I had just made a most imprudent marriage, when his death, which happened almost immediately upon his reverse of fortune, awoke me to the melancholy reality which stared me in the face.

"'In my distress I wrote to Robert Moncton, who had just commenced practice at his old office in Hatton Garden. He answered my appeal to his charity promptly, and gave me a seat in his office as engrossing clerk, with a very liberal salary which, I need not assure you, was most thankfully accepted by a person in my reduced circumstances. This place I filled entirely to his satisfaction for fifteen years, until I was the father of twelve children.

"'My salary was large, but, alas! it was the wages of sin. All Robert Moncton's dirty work was confided to my hands. I was his creature—the companion of his worst hours—and he paid me liberally for my devotion to his interests. But for all this, there were moments in my worthless life when better feelings prevailed; when I loathed the degrading trammels in which I was bound; and often, on the bosom of a dear and affectionate wife, I lamented bitterly my fallen state.

"'About this period Edward Moncton died, and Robert was appointed guardian to his orphan child. Property there was none —barely sufficient to pay the expenses of the funeral. Robert supplied from his own purse £50, towards the support of the young widow, until she could look about and obtain a situation as a day governess or a teacher in a school, for which she was eminently qualified.

"'I never shall forget the unnatural joy displayed by Robert on this melancholy occasion: "Thank God! William," said he, clapping me on the shoulder, after he had read the letter which poor Mrs. Moncton wrote to inform him of her sudden bereavement, 'Edward is dead. There is only one stumbling-block left in my path, and I will soon kick that out of the way.'

"'Three months had scarcely elapsed before I went to —— with Robert Moncton, to attend the funeral of his sister-in-law. The sight of the fine boy who acted as chief mourner in that mournful ceremony cut me to the heart. I was a father myself—a fond father—and I longed to adopt the poor, friendless child. But what could a man do who has a dozen of his own?

"'As we were on our road to ——, Robert had confided to me his plans for setting aside his nephew's claims to the estates and title of Moncton, in case you should die without a male heir. The secluded life which Mrs. Moncton had led since her marriage; her want of relatives to interest themselves in her behalf, and the dissipated habits of her husband, who had lost all his fine property at the gaming-table, made the scheme not only feasible, but presented few obstacles to its accomplishment.

"'Shocked at this piece of daring villainy, I dissembled my indignation, and while I appeared to acquiesce in his views, I secretly determined to befriend, if possible, the innocent child.

"'The night prior to the funeral, he called me into his private office, and after chatting over a matter of little consequence, he said to me in a careless manner:

""'By the by, Walters, Basset told me the other day, that you had taken a craze to go to America. This is your wife's doings, I suppose. I don't suffer Mrs. Moncton to settle such matters for me. But is it true?"

"'I said that it had been on my mind for a long time. The want of funds alone preventing me from emigrating with my family.'

""'If that is all, the want of money need not hinder you. But mind, Walters, I am not generous, I expect something for my gold. You have been faithful to me, and I am anxious to show you that I am not insensible to your merit. We are old friends, Walter—we understand each other; we are not troubled with nice scruples, and dare to call things by their right names. But to the point.

""'This boy of my brother's, as I was telling you, is a thorn in my side, which you can remove."

""'In what way?" said I, in a tone of alarm.

""'Don't look blue," he replied, and he laughed. "I kill with the tongue and the pen, and leave to fools the pistol and the knife. You must go to the parish of —— among the Derby hills, where Edward was married, and where he resided, enacting love in a cottage with his pretty, penniless bride, until after this boy, Geoffrey, was born; and subtract, if possible, the leaves from the church-register that contain these important entries. Do this with your usual address, and I will meet all the expenses of your intended emigration.'

"'The offer was tempting to a poor man, but I still hesitated, conjuring up a thousand difficulties which either awoke his mirth or scorn.

""'The only difficulty that I can find in the business," said he, "is your unwillingness to undertake it. The miserable old wretch employed as clerk in the church is quite superannuated. A small bribe will win him to your purpose, especially as Mr. Roche, the incumbent, is just now at the sea-side, whither he is gone in the delusive hope of curing old age. Possessed of these documents, I will defy the boy to substantiate his claims, provided that he lives to be a man; for I have carefully destroyed all the other documents which could lead to prove the legality of his title. The old gardener and his nurse must be persuaded to accompany you to America. Old Roche is on his last legs—from him I shall soon have nothing to fear. What do you say to my proposal—yes or no?"

""'Yes," I stammered out, "I will undertake it, as it is to be the last affair of the kind in which I mean to engage."

""'You will forget it," said he, "before you have half crossed the Atlantic, and can begin the world with a new character. I will give you five hundred pounds to commence with."

"'This iniquitous bargain concluded, I went down after the funeral to ——, on my mission. As my employer anticipated, a few shillings to the old clerk placed the church-register at my disposal, from which I carefully cut the leaves (which, in that quiet, out-of-the way hamlet, were not likely to be missed) which contained the entries. In a small hut among the hills I found the old gardener and his widowed daughter, who had been nurse to Geoffrey and his mother, whom I talked into a fever of enthusiasm about America, and the happy life which people led there, which ended in my engaging them, to accompany me. Good and valuable servants they both proved. They are since dead.'

"'And what became of the entries? Did you destroy them?'

"'I tried to do it, Sir Alexander, but it seemed as if an angel stayed my hand, and yielding to my impressions at the moment, I placed them carefully among my private papers. Here they are;' and taking from his breast-pocket an old-fashioned black leathern wallet, he placed them in my hand.

"'Here, too,' said he, 'is an affidavit, made by Michael Alzure on his dying bed, before competent witnesses, declaring that he was present with his daughter Mary, when the ceremony took place.'

"'This is enough,' said I, joyfully, shaking the old sinner heartily by the hand. 'The king shall have his own again. But how did you hoodwink that sagacious hawk, Robert Moncton?'

"'He was from home when I returned to London, attending the assizes at Bury. I found a letter from him containing a draft upon his banker for five hundred pounds, and requesting me to deposit the papers in the iron chest in the garret of which I had the key. I wrote in reply, that I had done so, and he was perfectly satisfied with my sincerity, which during fifteen years I had never given him the least cause to doubt.

"The next week, I sailed for the United States with my family, determined, from henceforth, to drop all connection with Robert Moncton, and to endeavour to obtain an honest living.

"'I am now a rich and prosperous man—my children are married and settled on good farms, in the same neighbourhood, and are in the enjoyment of the common comforts and many of the luxuries of life. Still, that little orphan boy haunted me: I could not be happy while I knew that I had been the means of doing him a foul injury, and I determined, as soon as I knew that the lad must be of age, to make a voyage to England, and place in your hands the proofs I held of his legitimacy.

"'Your powerful assistance, Sir Alexander, and these papers, will I trust restore to him his lawful place in society, and I am here to witness against Robert Moncton's villainy.'

"Well, Sir Geoffrey Moncton, that will be, what do you say to your old uncle's budget? Is not this news worth the postage? Worth throwing up one's cap and crying hurrah! and better still, dropping drown upon your knees in the solitude of your own chamber, and whispering in your clasped hands, 'Thank God! for all his mercies to me, a sinner?' If you omit the prayer, I have not omitted it for you; for most fervently I blessed the Almighty father for this signal instance of his love.

"I returned to the Park, so elated with the result of my journey, that I could scarcely sympathize in the grief of my poor girl, for the death of her foster-sister, which took place during my absence.

"Old Dinah is off. Perhaps gone somewhat before her time to her appointed place.

"It is useless for you to remain longer in Derbyshire, as we already possess all you want to know, and you must lose no time in commencing a suit against your uncle for conspiracy in order to defraud you out of your rights. Robert's character will never stand the test of this infamous exposure.

"My sweet Madge looks ill and delicate, and, like the old father, pines to see you again. You young scamp! you have taken a strange hold on the heart of your attached kinsman and faithful friend,

"ALEXANDER MONCTON."

I made my kind friend, Mrs. Hepburn, read over this important letter twice. It was the longest, I verily believe, that the worthy scribe ever penned in his life, and which nothing but his affection for me, could have induced him to write.

"God bless him!" I cried fervently, "how I long to see him again, and thank him from my very heart for all he has done for me!"

I was so elated, that I wanted to leave my bed instantly, and commence my journey to the Park. This was, however, but a momentary delusion: I was too weak, when I made the trial, to sit upright, or even to hold a pen, which was the most provoking of the two.

Mrs. Hepburn, at my earnest solicitation, wrote to Sir Alexander a long and circumstantial account of all that had befallen me since I left Moncton. That night was full of restless tossings to and fro. I sought rest, but found it not; nay, I could not even think with calmness, and the result was, as might have been expected, a great increase of fever, and for several days I was not only worse, but in considerable danger.

Nothing could be more tantalizing than this provoking relapse. A miserable presentiment of evil clouded my mind: my anxiety to write to Margaretta was painfully intense, and this was a species of communication which I could not very well convey through another.

To this unfortunate delay, I have attributed much of the sorrows of after years. Our will is free to plan. Our opportunities of action are in the hands of God. What I most ardently desired to do I was prevented from doing by physical weakness. How, then, can any man affirm that his destiny is in his own hands, when circumstances form a chain around him, as strong as fate, and the mind battles in vain against a host of trifles, despicable enough when viewed singly, but when taken in combination, possessing gigantic strength?

Another painful week wore slowly away, at the end of which I was able to sit up in a loose dressing-gown for several hours during the day.

I lost not a moment in writing to Margaretta directly I was able to hold a pen. I informed her of all that had passed between me and Catherine, and laid open my heart to her, without the least reserve. Deeming myself unworthy of her love, I left all to her generosity. I dispatched my letter with a thousand uncomfortable misgivings as to what effect it might produce upon the sensitive mind of my little cousin.

To write a long letter to George Harrison was the next duty I had to perform. But when I reflected on the delight which my communication could not fail to convey, this was not only an easy, but a delightful task. I had already arrived at the second closely written sheet, when a light tap at the door of the room announced the presence of Kate Lee.

"What, busy writing still, Geoffrey? What will honest Dan say to this rebellious conduct on the part of his patient? You must lay aside pens and paper for this day. Your face is flushed and feverish. Don't shake your head; my word is despotic in this house—I must be obeyed."

"Wait a few minutes, dear Miss Lee, and your will shall be absolute. It was because I am writing of you, that my letter has run to such an unconscionable length."

"Of me, Geoffrey?"

"Yes, of you, my charming friend."

"Nay, you are joking, Mr. Moncton. You would never distress me, by writing of me to strangers?"

"Strangers! oh no; but this is to one who is most dear to us both."

Catherine turned very pale.

"Geoffrey, I hope that you have not said anything that I could wish unsaid?"

"Do not look like a scared dove, sweet Kate. Have a little patience, and you shall read the letter."

"That is asking too much. I will trust to your honour—that innate sense of delicacy which I know you possess."

"You shall read the letter—I insist upon it. If you do not like it, I will write another. But you must sit down by me and listen to what I have to tell you, of my poor friend's history."

She turned her glistening eyes upon me, full of grateful thanks, and seated herself beside me on the couch. I then recounted to her the history which George had confided to me, though the narration was often interrupted by the sighs and tears of my attentive auditor.

After the melancholy tale was told, a long silence ensued. Poor Kate was too busy with her own thoughts to speak. I put the letter I had been writing into her hands, and retired to my own chamber, which opened into the one in which we were sitting, whilst she perused it. It was a simple statement of the facts related above. I had left him to draw from them what inference he pleased. When I returned an hour afterward to the sitting-room, which had been fitted up as such entirely for my accommodation, the windows opening into a balcony which ran along the whole front of the house, I found Kate leaning upon the railing, with the open letter still in her hand.

Her fine eyes were raised and full of tears, but she looked serene and happy, her beautiful face reminding me of an April sun just emerging from a soft fleecy cloud, which dimmed, only to increase by softening, the glory which it could not conceal.

"Well, dear Kate, may I finish my letter to George—for I must call him so still?"

"No."

"Why not," said I, surprised, and half angry.

"Because I mean to finish it myself. Will you give me permission?"

"By all means: it will make him so happy."

"And you are not jealous?" And as she said this, she bent upon me a curious and searching glance.

"Not now: a few weeks ago I should have been. To tell you the truth, dear Kate, I am too egotistical a fellow to love one who does not love me. I truly rejoice in the anticipated happiness of my friend."

Methought she looked a little disappointed, but recovering herself she added quickly—

"This is as it should be, yet I must own that my woman's vanity is a little hurt at the coolness of your philosophy. We all love power, Geoffrey, and do not like to lose it. Yet I am sincerely glad that you have conquered an attachment which would have rendered us both miserable. No fear of a broken heart in your case."

"Such things have been, and may be again, Kate, but I believe them to belong more to the poetry than the reality of life. Hearts are made of tough materials. They don't choose to break in the right place, and just when and where we want them."

She laughed, and asked when I thought I should be able to commence my journey to Moncton Park!

"In a few days I hope. I feel growing better every hour; my mind recovers elasticity with returning strength. But how I shall ever repay you, dear Miss Lee, and your excellent aunt, for your care and kindness puzzles me."

"Geoffrey, your accident has been productive of great good to us all; so say no more about it. I, for one, consider myself in your debt. You have made two friends, whom cruel destiny had separated, most happy."

CHAPTER XI.

A WELCOME AND AN UNWELCOME VISITOR.

Three days had scarcely elapsed, when I found myself mounted on my good steed, and gaily trotting along the road on my way to Moncton Park.

Honest Dan Simpson insisted on being my companion for the first stage. "Just," said he, "to take care of me, and see how I got along." I could gladly have dispensed with his company, for I longed to be alone; but to hurt the good fellow's feelings, would have been the height of ingratitude.

He had indignantly rejected the ample remuneration which Sir Alexander had remitted for his services.

"I took care of you for love, sir. It was no trouble, but a pleasure. As to money—I don't want it, I have saved a good pile for old age, and have neither wife nor child to give it to when I die. Lord! sir, I was afraid that you would take it ill, or I was going to ask you if you wanted any. I should have been proud to accommodate you, until you had plenty of your own."

I could have hugged the dear old man in my arms. Fortunately my being on horseback prevented such an excess. I turned to him to speak my thanks, but a choking in my throat prevented my uttering a word. He caught the glance of my moist eye, and dashed the dew, with his hard hand, from his own.

"I know what you would say, Mr. Geoffrey. But you need not say it—it would only make me feel bad."

"I shall never forget your kindness, Dan; but will always reckon you among my best friends."

"That's enough, sir: I'm satisfied, overpaid," and the true-hearted fellow rode close up to me and held out his hand. I shook it warmly. He turned his horse quickly round, and the sharp ringing of his hoofs on the rocky road told me that he was gone.

I rode slowly on; the day was oppressively warm, not a breath of air stirred the bushes by the road-side, or shook the dust from the tawny leaves which already had lost their tender green, and were embrowned beneath the hot gaze of the August noonday sun. Overcome by the heat, and languid from my long confinement to a sick room, I often checked my horse and sauntered slowly along, keeping the shady side of the road, and envying the cattle in the meadows standing mid leg in the shallow streams.

"There will surely be a storm before night," said I, looking wistfully up to the cloudless sky, which very much resembled Job's description of a molten looking-glass. "I feel the breath of the tempest in this scorching air. A little rain would lay the dust, and render to-morrow's journey less fatiguing."

My soliloquy was interrupted by the sharp click of a horse's hoofs behind me, and presently his rider passed me at full speed. A transient glance at the stranger's face made me suddenly recoil.

It was Robert Moncton.

He looked pale and haggard, and his countenance wore an unusual appearance of anxiety and care. He did not notice me, and checking my horse, I felt relieved when a turning in the road hid him from my sight.

His presence appeared like a bad omen. A heavy gloom sunk upon my spirits, and I felt half inclined to halt at the small village I was approaching and rest until the heat of the day had subsided, and I could resume my journey in the cool of the evening.

Ashamed of such weakness, I resolutely turned my face from every house of entertainment I passed, and had nearly cleared the long straggling line of picturesque white-washed cottages, which composed the larger portion of the village, when the figure of a gentleman pacing to and fro, in front of a decent-looking inn, arrested my attention. There was something in the air and manner of this person, which appeared familiar to me. He raised his head as I rode up to the door. The recognition was mutual.

"Geoffrey Moncton!"

"George Harrison! Who would have thought of meeting you in this out of the way place?"

"There is an old saying, Geoffrey—talk of the Devil and he is sure to appear. I was thinking of you at the very moment, and raising my eyes saw you before me."

"Ay, that is one of the mysteries of mind, which has still to be solved," said I, as I dismounted from my horse and followed George into the house. "I am so heartily glad to see you, old fellow," cried I, directly we were alone: "I have a thousand things to say to you, which could not be crowded into the short compass of a letter."

"Hush! don't speak so loud," and he glanced suspiciously round. "These walls may have ears. I know, that they contain one, whom you would not much like to trust with your secrets."

"How—is *he* here?"

"You know whom I mean?"

"Robert Moncton? He passed me on the road."

"Did he recognize you?"

"I think not. His hat was slouched over his forehead; his eyes bent moodily on the ground. Besides, George, I am so greatly altered by my long illness; I am surprised that you knew me again."

"Love and hatred, are great sharpeners of the memory. It is as hard to forget an enemy as a friend. But to tell you the truth, Geoffrey, I had to look at you twice before I knew who you were. But come up-stairs—I have a nice snug room, where we can chat in private whilst dinner is preparing."

"I should like to know what brings Robert Moncton this road," said I, flinging my weary length upon a crazy old sofa, which occupied a place in the room more for ornament than use, and whose gay chintz cover, like charity, hid a multitude of defects. "No good I fear."

"I cannot exactly tell. There is some new scheme in the wind. Harry Bell, who fills my old place in his office, informed me that a partial reconciliation had taken place between father and son. This was by letter, for no personal interview had brought them together. Theophilus was on his way to Moncton, and appointed the old rascal to meet him somewhere on the road. What the object of their meeting may be, time alone can discover. Perhaps, to discover Dinah North's place of concealment, or to ascertain if the old hag be dead. Her secresy on some points of their history is a matter of great moment."

"They are a pair of precious scoundrels, and their confederation portends little good to me."

"You need not care a rush for them now, Geoffrey, you are beyond the reach of their malice. Moncton is not aware of the return of Walters. This circumstance will be a death-blow to his ambitious hopes. How devoutly they must have wished you in Heaven during your illness."

"At one time, I almost wished myself there."

"You were not too ill to forget your friend, Geoffrey," and he rose and pressed my hand warmly between his own. "How can I thank you sufficiently for your disinterested kindness. By your generous sacrifice of self you have made me the happiest of men. I am now on my way to Elm Grove to meet one, whom I never hoped to meet in this world again."

"Say nothing about it, George. The sacrifice may be less disinterested than you imagine: I no longer regret it, and am heartily glad that I have been instrumental to this joyful change in your prospects. But why, my good fellow, did you conceal from me the name of the beloved. Had you candidly told me who the lady was, I should not have wounded by my coldness a dear and faithful heart."

"Your mind was so occupied by the image of Kate Lee that I dared not."

"It would have saved me a deal of misery."

"And destroyed our friendship."

"You don't know me, George; honesty would have been the best policy, as it always is, in all cases. I could have given up Kate when I knew that she loved, and was beloved by my friend. Your want of candour and confidence may have been the means of destroying Margaretta Moncton."

"Do not look so dreadfully severe, Geoffrey. I admit that truth is the best guide of all our actions. It was my love for you, however, which led me to disguise the name of Catherine Lee. You don't know what a jealous fellow you are, and at that time you were too much excited and too ill to hear the truth. What I did for the best has turned out, as it sometimes does, quite contrary to my wishes. You must forgive me, Geoffrey. It is the first time I ever deceived you, and it will be the last."

He took my hand and looked earnestly into my face, with those mild, melancholy eyes. To be angry long with him was impossible. It was far more easy to be angry with myself; so, I told him that I forgave him from my very heart, and would no longer harbour against him an unkind thought.

I was still far from well, low-spirited and out of humour with myself and the whole world. I felt depressed with the mysterious and unaccountable dejection of mind, which often precedes some unlooked-for calamity.

In vain were all my efforts to rouse myself from this morbid lethargy. The dark cloud which weighed down my spirits would not be dispelled. I strove to be gay; the laugh died upon my lips or was choked by involuntary sighs. George, who was anxiously watching my countenance, rose and walked to the window; and, tired of my uneasy position on the hard, crazy, old sofa, and willing to turn the current of my thoughts from flowing in such a turbid bed, I followed his example.

We stood for a while in silence, watching the groups which occasionally gathered beneath the archway of the little inn, to discuss the news of the village.

"You are not well, Geoffrey. Your journey has fatigued you. Lie down and rest for a few hours."

"Sleep is out of the question in my present feverish state. I will resume my journey."

"What, in the face of the storm which is rapidly gathering! Do you see that heavy cloud in the north-west?"

"I am not afraid of thunder."

"It has a particular effect upon some people. It gives me an intolerable headache, hours before it is even apparent in the heavens. To this cause I attribute your sudden depression of spirits."

I shook my head sceptically.

"Then, do tell me, dear Geoffrey, what it is that disturbs you?"

"My own thoughts. Do not laugh, George. These things to the sufferer are terrible realities. I am oppressed by melancholy anticipations of evil. A painful consciousness of approaching sorrow. I have experienced this often before, but never to such an extent as to-day. Let me have my own way. It is good for me to combat with the evil genius alone."

"I think not. Duty compels us to combat with such feelings. The indulgence of them tends to shake our reliance on the mercy of God, and to render us unhappy and discontented."

"This is one of the mysteries of mind which we cannot comprehend. The links which unite the visible with the invisible world. But whether they have their origin from above or beneath is, to me, very doubtful; unless such presentiments operate as a warning to shun impending danger.

"I hear no admonitory voice within. All is dark, still and heavy, like the black calm that slumbers in the dense folds of yon thundercloud; as if the mind was suddenly deprived of all vital energy, and crouched beneath an overwhelming consciousness of horror."

George gave me a sudden sidelong scrutinizing glance, as if he suspected my recent accident had impaired my reason.

A vivid flash of lightning, followed by a sudden crash of thunder, made us start some paces back from the window, and a horseman dashed at full speed into the inn yard.

Another blinding flash—another roar of thunder, which seemed to fill the whole earth and heavens, made me involuntarily close my eyes, when an exclamation from George—"Good heavens, what an escape!"—made me as quickly hurry to the window.

The lightning had struck down the horse and rider whom we had before observed. The nobler animal alone was slain.

The avenging bolt of heaven had passed over and left the head of the rider, Theophilus Moncton, unscathed!

Livid with recent terror, and vexed with the loss of the fine animal at his feet, he cast a menacing glance at the lowering sky above, and bidding the ostler with an oath (which sounded like double blasphemy in our ears) to take care of the saddle and bridle, he entered the inn, shaking the mud and rain from his garments, and muttering indistinct curses on his ill-luck.

"The blasphemous wretch!" cried I, drawing a long breath. "Bad as the father is, he is an angel when compared with the son."

"Geoffrey, he is what the father has made him. I would give much to witness the meeting."

"You would see a frightful picture of human guilt and depravity. Half his fortune would scarcely bribe me to witness such a revolting scene."

The rain was now pouring in torrents, and one inky hue had overspread the whole heavens. Finding that we were likely to be detained some hours, George ordered dinner, and we determined to make ourselves as comfortable as circumstances would admit.

All our efforts to provoke mirth, however, proved abortive. The silence of our meal was alone broken by the dull clattering of knives and forks, and the tinkling of the bell to summon the brisk waiter to bring wine and draw the cloth. But if we were silent, an active spirit was abroad in the house, and voices in loud and vehement altercation in the room adjoining, arrested our attention.

The muttered curse, the restless, impatient walking to and fro, convinced us that the parties were no other than Robert Moncton and his son, and that their meeting was not likely to have a very amicable termination. At length, the voice of my uncle in a terrible state of excitement, burst forth with this awful sentence:

"I discard you, sir! From this day you cease to be my son. Go, and take my curse along with you! Go to ——! and may we never meet in time or eternity again."

With a bitter, sneering laugh the disinherited replied: "In heaven we shall never meet; on earth, perhaps, we may meet too soon. In the place to which you have so unceremoniously sent me, I can perceive some lingering remains of paternal affection—that where you are, I may be also."

"Hold your tongue, sir. Dare you to bandy words with me?"

"It would be wisdom in you, my most righteous progenitor, to bribe me to do so, when you know how much that tongue can reveal."

Another sneering derisive laugh from the son, of fiendish exultation, and a deep, hollow groan from the father, and the unhallowed conference was over.

Some one passed the door with rapid steps. I talked to the window as Theophilus emerged into the court-yard below. He raised his eyes to the window: I met their dull, leaden stare; he started and stopped; I turned contemptuously away.

Presently after we heard him bargaining for a horse to carry him as far as York on his way to London.

"I don't envy Robert Moncton's feelings," said George. "What can have been the cause of this violent quarrel?"

"It may spring from several causes. His son's marriage alone would be sufficient to exasperate a man of his malignant disposition. But look, Harrison, the clouds are parting in the west. The moon rises early; and we shall have a lovely night after the rain for our journey to York."

"Our—I was going by the coach which passes through the village in an hour to Elm Grove. But now I think of it, I will postpone my visit until the morrow, and accompany you a few miles on your way."

"I should be delighted with your company, George, but——"

"You would rather be alone, nursing these gloomy thoughts?"

"Not exactly. But it will postpone your visit to Miss Lee."

"Only a few hours; and as I wrote yesterday and never mentioned my visit, which was a sudden whim (one of your *odd* presentiments, Geoffrey, which seemed to compel me almost against my will to come here) she cannot be disappointed. To tell you the truth, I did not like the look with which your cousin recognized you. When rogues are abroad it behoves honest men to keep close together. I am determined to see you safe to York."

I was too much pleased with the proposal to raise any obstacles in the way. We fell into cheerful conversation, and whilst watching the clearing up of the weather, we saw Robert Moncton mount his horse and ride out of the inn-yard.

"The sun is breaking through the clouds, George. It is time we were upon the road."

"With all my heart," said he; and a few minutes after we were upon our journey.

The freshness of the air after the heavy rains, the delicious perfume of the hedge-rows, and the loud clear notes of the blackbird resounding from the bosky dells in the lordly plantations skirting the road, succeeded in restoring my animal spirits.

Nothing could exceed the tranquillity of the lovely evening. George often checked his horse and broke out into enthusiastic exclamations of delight whilst pointing out to me the leading features in the beautiful country through which we were travelling.

"Where are your gloomy forebodings now, Geoffrey?" said he.

"This glorious scene has well-nigh banished them," I replied. "Nature has always such an exhilarating effect upon my mind that I can hardly feel miserable while the sun shines."

George turned towards me his kindling eyes and animated countenance.

"Geoffrey, I have not felt so happy as I do this evening, since I was a little, gay, light-hearted boy. I could sing aloud in the joyousness of hope and pleasing anticipation. In this respect my feelings during the day have been quite the opposite of yours. I reproach myself for not being able to sympathize in your nervously depressed state of mind."

"Your being sad, George, would not increase my cheerfulness. The quiet serenity of the hour has operated upon me like a healing balm. I can smile at my superstitious fears, now that the dark cloud is clearing from my mind."

Thus we rode on, chatting with the familiarity of long-tried friendship, discussing our past trials, present feelings, and future prospects, until the moon rose brightly on our path; and we pushed our horses to a quicker pace, in order to reach the city before midnight.

The road we were travelling had been cut through a steep hill. The banks on either side were very high, and crowned with plantations of pine and fir, which cast into deep shadow the space between. The hill was terminated by a large deep gravel pit, through the centre of which our path lay; and the opposite rise of the hill, which was destitute of trees, lay gleaming brightly in the moonshine.

As we gained the wood-crowned height, we perceived a horseman slowly riding down the steep before us. His figure was so blended with the dark shadows of the descending road, that the clicking of his horse's hoofs, and the moving mass of deeper shade alone proclaimed his proximity.

"This is a gloomy spot, George. I wish we were fairly out of it."

"Afraid, Geoffrey—and two to one?"

"No, not exactly afraid; but this spot would be lonely at noonday. Look—look! George, what makes that man so suddenly check his horse as he gains the centre of the pit and emerges into the moonlight?"

"Silence!" cried George. "That was the report of a pistol. Follow me!"

We spurred our horses to full speed and galloped down the hill.

The robbers, if indeed any were near, had disappeared, and we found the man whom we had previously observed, rolling on the ground in great agony, and weltering in blood.

Dismounting from our horses, we ran immediately to his assistance. He raised his head as we approached, and said in a low hollow voice, "I am shot—I know the rascal—he cannot escape. Raise my head, I feel choking—a little higher. The wound may not be mortal, I may live to be revenged upon him yet."

The sound of that voice—the sight of those well-known features, rendered me powerless. I stood mute and motionless, staring upon the writhing and crushed wretch before me, unable to render him the least assistance.

It was my uncle who lay bleeding there, slain by some unknown hand. A horrible thought flashed through my brain; a ghastly sickness came over me and I stifled the unnatural supposition.

In the meanwhile Harrison had succeeded in raising Mr. Moncton into a sitting posture, and had partly ascertained the nature of his wound. Whilst thus employed, the moon shone full upon his face, and my uncle, uttering a cry of terror, fell prostrate on the ground, whilst the blood gushed in a dark stream from his wounded shoulder.

"Geoffrey," exclaimed George, beckoning me to come to him, "don't stand shaking there like a person in an ague fit. Something must be done, and that immediately, or your uncle will die on the road. Mount the high bank, and see if you can discover any dwelling nigh at hand, to which he can be conveyed."

His voice broke the horrid trance in which my senses were bound. I sprang up the steep side of the gravel pit, and saw before me a marshy meadow, and not far from the road, a light glimmered from a cabin window. It was a wretched-looking place, but the only habitation in sight, nearer than the village, whose church spire, about two miles distant, glimmered in the moonbeams. Turning our horses loose to graze in the meadow, we lifted a gate from the hinges, and placing the now insensible man upon this rough litter, which we covered with our travelling-cloaks, we succeeded with much difficulty, and after a considerable lapse of time, in reaching the miserable hovel.

On the approach of footsteps, the persons within extinguished the light, and for some time we continued rapping at the door without receiving any answer.

I soon lost all patience, and began to hallo and shout in the hope of provoking attention.

Another long pause.

"Open the door," cried I, "a man has been shot on the road: he will die without assistance."

A window in the thatch slowly unclosed, and a hoarse female voice croaked forth in reply: "What concern is that of mine? Who are you who disturb honest folk at this hour of the night with your drunken clamours? My house is my castle. Begone, I tell you! I will not come down to let you in."

"Dinah North," said Harrison, solemnly, "I have a message for you, which you dare not gainsay—I command you to unbar the door and receive us instantly."

This speech was answered by a wild shrill cry, more resembling the howl of a tortured dog than any human sound. I felt the blood freeze in my veins. Harrison whispered in my ear: "She will obey my summons, which she believes not one of earth. Stay with your uncle, while I ride forward to the village to procure medical aid, and make a deposition before the magistrate of what has occurred. Don't let the fiend know that I am alive. It is of the utmost importance to us all, that she should still believe me dead."

I tried to detain him, not much liking my present position; but he had vanished, and shortly after I heard the clatter of his horse's hoofs galloping at full speed towards the town.

What a fearful termination of my gloomy presentiments, thought I, as I looked down at the livid face and prostrate form of Robert Moncton.

"Where will this frightful scene end?" I exclaimed.

The gleam of a light flashed across the broken casement; the next moment Dinah North stood before me.

"Geoffrey Moncton, is this you?" There was another voice that spoke to me —a voice from the grave. "Where is your companion?"

"I am alone with the dead," said I, pointing to the body. "Look there!"

She held up the light and bent over that insensible bleeding mass, and looked long, and I thought triumphantly, at the ghastly face of the accomplice in all her crimes. Then turning her hollow eyes on me, she said calmly:

"Did you murder him?"

"No, thank God! I am guiltless of his blood; but he seems to know the hand that dealt the blow."

"Ha, ha!" shrieked the hag, "my dream was true—my horrible dream. Even so, last night, I saw Robert Moncton weltering in his blood, and my poor Alice was wiping the death-damps from his brow; and I saw more—more, but it was a sight for the damned—a sight which cannot be repeated to mortal ears. Yes, Robert Moncton, it is all up with you; we have sinned together and must both drink of that fiery cup. I know the worst now."

"Hush! he moves—he still lives. He may yet recover. Let us carry him into the house."

"He has troubled the earth and your father's house long enough, Geoffrey Moncton," said the strange woman, in a softened, and I thought, melancholy tone. "It is time that both he and I received the reward of our misdeeds."

She assisted me to carry the body into the house, and stripping off the clothes, we laid it upon a low flock bed, which occupied one corner of the miserable apartment, over which she threw a coarse woollen coverlid.

She then examined the wound with a critical eye, and after washing it with brandy she said that the ball could be extracted, and she thought that the wound was not mortal and might be cured.

Tearing his neckcloth into bandages, she succeeded in staunching the blood, and diluting some of the brandy with water, she washed the face of the wounded man, and forced a few spoonfuls down his throat. Drawing a long, deep sigh, Robert Moncton unclosed his eyes. For some minutes, they rested unconsciously upon us. Recollection slowly returned, and recoiling from the touch of that abhorrent woman he closed them again and groaned heavily.

"We have met, Robert, in an evil hour. The friendship of the wicked brings no comfort in the hour of death or in the day of judgment."

"Avaunt witch! The sight of your hideous face is worse than the pangs of death. Death," he repeated slowly—"I am not near death—I will not die—I cannot die."

"You dare not!" said Dinah, in a low, malignant whisper. "Is this cowardly dastard, the proud, wealthy Robert Moncton, who thought to build up his house by murder and treachery? Methinks this is a noble apartment and a fitting couch for the body of Sir Robert Moncton to lie in state."

"Mocking fiend! what pleasure can you find in my misery?"

"Much, much—oh, how much! It is not fair that I should bear the tortures of the damned alone. Since the death of the only thing I ever loved I have had strange thoughts and terrible visions; restless, burning nights and fearful days. But I cannot repent or wish undone that which is done. I can neither weep nor pray; I can only curse—bitterly curse thee and thine! I rejoice to see this hour —to know that before I depart to your Master and mine, the vengeance of my soul will be satisfied."

"Geoffrey, I implore you to drive that beldame from the room. The sight of her hideous face and her ominous croaking will drive me mad."

"Uncle, do not exhaust your strength by answering her. She is not in her right senses. In a few minutes my friend will return with surgical aid, and we will get you removed to more comfortable lodgings in the village."

"Do not deceive yourselves," returned Dinah: "from the bed on which he now lies, the robber and murderer will never rise again. As he has sown so must he reap. He deserves small kindness at your hands, Geoffrey Moncton. You should rather rejoice that the sting of the serpent is drawn, and that he can hurt you and yours no more."

"Alas!" returned I, taking the hand of the wretched sufferer in mine, "how much rather would I see him turn from his evil deeds and live!"

"God bless you! Geoffrey," sobbed forth my miserable uncle, bursting into tears: perhaps the first he ever shed in his life. "Deeply have I sinned against you, noble, generous boy. Can you forgive me for my past cruelty?"

"I can—I do; and should it please God to restore you to health, I will prove the truth of what I say by deeds, not words."

"Do not look so like your father, Geoffrey. His soul speaks to me through your eyes. Your kindness heaps coals of fire upon my head. It would give me less torture to hear you curse than pray for me."

"Pray for yourself, uncle. I have never attended to these things as I ought to have done. I am punished now, when I have no word of comfort or instruction for you."

"Pray!" and he drew a long sigh. "My mother died when Ned and I were boys. We soon forgot the prayers she taught us. My father's God was Mammon. He taught me early to worship at the same shrine. No, Geoffrey, no: it is too late to pray. I feel—I know that I am lost. I have no part or lot in the Saviour—no love for God, in whom I never believed until this fatal hour.

"I have injured you, Geoffrey, and am willing to make all the reparation in my power by restoring to you those rights which I have laboured so hard to set aside."

"Spare yourself, uncle, the painful relation. Let no thought on that score divert your mind from making its peace with God. Walters has returned, and the documents necessary to prove my legitimacy are in Sir Alexander's hands."

"Walters returned!" shrieked my uncle. "Both heaven and hell conspire against me. What a tale can he unfold."

"Ay, and what a sequel can I add to it," said Dinah, rising from her seat, and standing before him like one of the avenging furies. "Listen to me, Geoffrey Moncton, for it shall yet be told."

"Spare me! cruel woman, in mercy spare me. Is not your malice sufficiently gratified to see me humbled to the dust?"

"Ah! if your villainy had proved successful, and you were revelling in wealth and splendour, instead of grovelling there beneath the lash of an awakened conscience, where would be your repentance? What would *then* become of Geoffrey Moncton's claims to legitimacy? I trow he would remain a bastard to the end of his days."

"Geoffrey, for God's sake bid that woman hold her venomous tongue. I feel faint and sick with her upbraidings."

"He is fainting," said I, turning to Dinah. "Allow him to die in peace."

"You are a fool to feel the least trouble about him," said Dinah. "There, he is again insensible; our efforts to bring him to his senses will only make matters worse. Listen to me, Geoffrey Moncton, I have a burden on my conscience I would fain remove, and which it is necessary that you should know. Remember what I told you when we last met. That the next time we saw each other, my secret and yours would be of equal value."

CHAPTER XII.

DINAH'S CONFESSION.

"It is an ill wind, they say, Geoffrey Moncton, which blows no good to any one. Had the son of Sir Alexander Moncton lived, you would have retained your original insignificance. It is from my guilt that you derive a clear title to the lands and honours which by death he lost."

I know not why, but as she said this, a cold chill crept through me. I almost wished that she would leave the terrible tale she had to tell untold. I felt that whatever its import might be, that it boded me no good. My situation was intensely exciting, and made me alive to the most superstitious impressions. It was altogether the most important epoch in my life.

Seated at the foot of that miserable bed, the ghastly face of the wounded man, just revealed by the sickly light of a miserable candle, looked stark, rigid, and ghost-like, to all outward appearance, already dead. And that horrible hag, with her witch-like face, with its grim smile, standing between me and the clear beams of the moon, which bathed in a silvery light the floor of that squalid room, and threw fantastic arabesques over the time-stained walls, glanced upon me like some foul visitant from the infernal abyss.

The hour was solemn midnight, when the dead are said to awake in their graves, and wander forth until the second crowing of the bird of dawn. I felt its mysterious influence steal over my senses, and rob me of my usual courage, and I leant forward, to shut out the ghastly scene, and covered my face with my hands.

Every word which Dinah uttered fell upon my ear with terrible distinctness, as she continued her revelations of the past.

"My daughter, Rachel, by some strange fatality had won the regard of her delicate rival, Lady Moncton, who seemed to feel a perverse pleasure in loading her with favours. Whether she knew of the attachment which had existed between her and Sir Alexander is a secret. Perhaps she did not, and was only struck with the beauty and elegance of the huntsman's wife, which was certainly very unusual in a person of her humble parentage. Be that as it may, she deemed her worthy of the highest trust which one woman, can repose in another—the charge of her infant son, and that son the heir of a vast estate.

"Rachel was not insensible to the magnitude of the confidence reposed in her; and for the first six months of the infant's life, she performed her duty conscientiously, and bestowed upon her nurse-child the most devoted care.

"Robert Moncton came to the Hall at this time to receive the rents of the estate for Sir Alexander—for he was his man of business. He saw the child, and perceived that it was a poor, fragile, puling thing; the thought entered his wicked heart, that if this weakly scion of the old family tree were removed, his son would be heir to the title and lands of Moncton.

"I don't know what argument he made use of to win Rachel to his purpose. I was living with him at the time as his housekeeper; for the wife he had married was a poor, feeble-minded creature—the mere puppet of his imperious will, and a very indifferent manager. But she loved him, and at that period he was a very handsome man, and had the art of hiding his tyrannical temper, by assuming before strangers a pleasing, dignified manner, which imposed on every person who was not acquainted with the secrets of the domestic prison-house.

"Rachel consented to make away with the child; but on the very night she had set apart for the perpetration of the deed, God smote her own lovely boy upon the breast, and the tears of the distracted mother awoke in her mind a consciousness of the terrible sin she had premeditated.

"To hearts like Robert Moncton's and mine this circumstance would not have deterred us from our purpose; but Rachel was not like us, hardened in guilt or bad, and unknown to us both she reared the young heir of Moncton as her own.

"It was strange that neither of us suspected the fact.

"I might have known, from the natural antipathy I felt for the child, that he was not of my flesh and blood; but God hid it from me, till Rachel informed me on her death-bed of the deception she had practised.

"It was an important secret, and I determined to make use of it to extort money from Robert Moncton, when the child should be old enough to attract his attention. I owed him a long grudge, and this gave me power to render him restless and miserable. Thus I suffered George Moncton to live, to obtain a two-fold object—the gratification of Avarice and Revenge.

"In spite of neglect and harsh treatment, which were inseparable from the deep-rooted hatred I bore him on his parents' account, the hand of Heaven was extended over the injured child. He out-grew the feeble delicacy of his infancy, and when he had attained his fourth year, was a beautiful and intelligent boy.

"His father, as if compelled by powerful natural instinct, lavished upon him the most abundant marks of favour. Lady Moncton's love was that of a doting mother, which increased up to the period of her death.

"The death of Lady Moncton, and that of Roger Mornington, followed quickly upon each other, and all my old hopes revived, when Sir Alexander renewed his attentions to my daughter. But vain are the expectations of the wicked. Bitter experience has taught me (though it took me a long life to learn that lesson) that man cannot contend with God; and my beautiful Rachel died in her prime, just when my fondest expectations seemed on the point of realization.

"Years fled on—years of burning disappointment and ungratified passion. The little girl Rachel left to my care was handsome, clever and affectionate, and I loved her with a fierce love, such as I never felt before for anything of earth—and she loved me—a creature from whose corrupted nature, all living things seemed to start with abhorrence. I watched narrowly the young heir of Moncton, who led that smiling rose-bud by the hand, and loved her too, but not as I could have wished him to love her.

"Had I seen the least hope of his ever forming an attachment for his beautiful playmate, how different would have been my conduct towards him!

"Alice, was early made acquainted with the secret of his birth, and was encouraged by me, to use every innocent blandishment towards him, and even to hint that he was not her brother, in order to awaken a tenderer passion in his breast.

"His heart remained as cold as ice. His affections for Alice never exceeded the obligations of nature, due to her as his sister. They were not formed for each other and, again disappointed in my ambitious hopes, I vowed his destruction. At this time Sir Alexander sent him to school at York, and the man who lies grovelling on that bed, was made acquainted with his existence."

A heavy groan from Robert Moncton interrupted for a few minutes the old woman's narrative. She rose from her seat, took the lamp from the table, and bending over the sorry couch, regarded the rigid marble features of my uncle, with the same keen scrutiny that she had looked upon me in the garret of the old house in Hatton Garden.

"It was but a passing pang," said she, resuming her seat. "His ear is closed to all intelligible sounds."

I thought otherwise, but after rocking herself to and fro on her seat for a short space, she again fixed upon me her dark, searching, fiery eyes, and resumed her tale:—

"Robert Moncton bore the intelligence with more temper than I expected. Nor did he then propose any act of open violence towards the innocent object of our mutual hatred, but determined to destroy him in a more deliberate and less dangerous way. At that time I was not myself eager for his death, for my poor deluded, lost Alice, had not then formed the ill-fated attachment to Theophilus Moncton, which terminated in her broken heart and early grave— and which, in fact, has proved the destruction of all, and rendered the house of the destroyer as desolate as my own.

"At first I could not believe that the attachment of my poor girl to Theophilus was sincere, but when I was at length convinced that both were in earnest, my long withered hopes revived. I saw her in idea, already mistress of the Hall, and often in private called her Lady Moncton.

"I despised the surly wretch, whom unfortunately she only loved too well, and looked upon his union with my grandchild as a necessary evil, through which she could alone reach the summit of my ambitious wishes.

"In the meanwhile, Alice played her cards so well that she and her lover were privately married—she binding herself by a solemn promise, not to divulge the secret, even to me, until a fitting opportunity. After a few months, her situation attracted my attention; and I accused her of having been betrayed by her fashionable paramour.

"She denied the charge—was obstinate and violent, and much bitter language passed between us. Just at this period, young Mornington returned to us, a ruined man. He fell sick, and both Alice and myself hoped that his disease would terminate fatally. In this we were disappointed. He slowly and surely recovered in spite of our coldness and neglect.

"Before he was able to leave his bed, Robert Moncton, who had discovered his victim's retreat, paid us a visit. Me, he cajoled, by promising to give his consent to his son's marriage with Alice, but only on condition of our uniting to rid him for ever of the man who stood between him and the long-coveted estates and title of Moncton. I, for my part, was easily entreated, for our interests were too closely united in his destruction, for me to raise any objections.

"Alice, however, was a novice in crime, and she resisted his arguments with many tears, and it was not until he threatened to disinherit her husband, if he ever dared to speak to her again, that she reluctantly consented to administer the fatal draught which Robert prepared with his own hands."

There was a long pause; I thought I heard the sound of horses' hoofs in the distance. Dinah heard it too, and hastened to conclude her narrative.

"Yes, George Moncton died in the bloom of life, the victim of treachery from the very morning of his days. But the cry of the innocent blood has gone up to the throne of God, and terrible vengeance has pursued his murderers.

"When I discovered that Alice was the lawful wife of Theophilus Moncton, and that the child she carried, if it proved a son, would be Sir Alexander's heir, I made a journey to London, to communicate the fact to Robert Moncton, and to force him to acknowledge her publicly as his daughter-in-law.

"He would not believe me on my oath; and declared that it was only another method to extort money. I produced the proofs. He vowed that they were base forgeries, and tore the documents, trampling them under his feet;

and it was only when I threatened to expose the murder of his cousin, that he condescended to listen to reason.

"It was then for the first time I heard of your existence, and a new and unforeseen enemy seemed to start up and defy me to my teeth.

"Robert Moncton laughed at my fears, and told me how ingeniously he had contrived to brand you with the stigma of illegitimacy. He could not however lull my fears to rest, until I was satisfied that Walters had really placed the stolen certificates in the iron chest in your garret—and late as it was, we went to assure ourselves of the fact."

"Oh, how well I remember that dreadful visit," said I—"and the horrible dream which preceded it."

"You were awake, then?"

"Yes—awake with my eyes shut—and heard all that passed."

"A true Moncton," and she shook her palsied head. "The devil is in you all. You know then, that our search was fruitless, and I returned to Moncton with the conviction, that we were destined to be defeated in our machinations.

"Six months after these events, Alice gave birth to a son, and was greatly cheered by the news, which reached her through one of the servants at the Hall, that her husband had returned from Italy, and was in London."

"The rest of her melancholy history is known to me," said I. "It was my arm that lifted her from the water when she attempted to destroy herself. Oh, miserable and guilty woman, what have you gained by all your deep-laid schemes of villainy? As to you, Dinah North, the gibbet awaits you—and your prospects beyond the grave are more terrible still."

"Dinah North will never die beneath the gaze of an insolent mob," said the old woman with a sullen laugh. "A few months ago, Geoffrey Moncton, and I would have suffered the rack, before I would have confessed to you aught that might render you a service, but the kindness you showed to my unhappy grandchild, awoke in my breast a feeling towards you foreign to my nature. I have been a terrible enemy to your house. But you, at least, should regard me as a friend. Had George Moncton lived, what would become of your claims to rank and fortune?"

"Dinah, he does live!" and the conviction that I was penniless, a poor dependent upon a noble house, instead of being the expectant heir, pressed at that moment painfully on my heart. "See," I continued, as the door opened, and George attended by several persons entered the house, "he is here to assert his lawful claims. The grave has given up its dead."

The same wild shriek which burst so frightfully on my ears, when George first addressed the old woman, ran through the apartment.

"Constables, do your duty," said George. "Instantly secure that woman."

As he spoke, the light was suddenly extinguished, and we were left in darkness. Before the hurry and bustle of rekindling it was over, Dinah North had disappeared, and all search after her proved fruitless.

CHAPTER XIII.
RETRIBUTIVE JUSTICE.

Robert Moncton had lain in a stupor for the last hour. The surgeon whom George had brought with him from the village, after carefully examining the wound, to my surprise, declared that it was mortal, and that the sufferer could not be removed, as his life must terminate in a few hours. During the extraction of the bullet and the dressing of the wound, Robert Moncton recovered his senses and self-possession, and heard his doom with a glassy gaze of fixed despair. Then, with a deep sigh, he asked if a lawyer were present, as he wished to make his will, and set his affairs in order before he died.

George had brought with him a professional gentleman, the clergyman, and one of the chief magistrates in the village. He now introduced to his notice the Rev. Mr. Chapman, and Mr. Blake the solicitor.

"When I require your offices," he said, addressing the former gentleman, "I will send for you. Such comfort as you can give in the last hour, will not atone for the sins of a long life. This is one of the fallacies to which men cling when they can no longer help themselves. They will, however, find it a broken reed when called upon to pass through the dark valley.

"With you, sir," shaking hands with Mr. Blake, "my business lies. Clear the room till this matter is settled: I wish us to be alone."

The clergyman, finding that he would not be listened to, mounted his horse and rode away. George and I gladly availed ourselves of the opportunity of leaving for a while the gloomy chamber of death, and taking a turn in the fresh air. We wandered forth into the clear night; the blessed and benignant aspect of nature, forming, as it ever does, a solemn, holy contrast with the turbulent, restless spirit of man. Nature has her storms and awful convulsions, but the fruits are fertility, abundance, rest. The fruits of our malignant passions—sin, disease, mental and physical death.

My blighted prospects, in spite of all my boasted disinterestedness, weighed heavily on my heart. I tried to rejoice in my friend's good fortune, but human nature with all its sins and weaknesses prevailed. I was not then a Christian, and could scarcely be expected to prefer the good of my neighbour to my own.

Bowed down and humbled by the consciousness of all I had lost, I should had I been alone have shamed my manhood, and found relief in tears.

"Dear Geoffrey, why so silent?" said George, wringing my hand with his usual warmth: "Have you no word for your friend? This night has been one of severe trial. God knows how deeply I sympathize in your feelings! But cheer up, my dear fellow; better and brighter moments are at hand."

"No, no, not for me," returned I, almost choking. "I am one of the unlucky ones; no good can ever happen to me. My hopes are blighted for ever. It is only you, George Moncton, who, in this dark hour, have reason to rejoice."

He stopped and grasped my arm. "What do you mean, Geoffrey, when you call me by that name?"

"That it belongs to you."

"To me! Has Dinah made any confession?"

"She has. Have a little patience, George, till I can collect my scattered thoughts, and tell you all."

I then communicated to him the conversation that had passed between Dinah and myself, though my voice often trembled with emotion, and I could scarcely repress my tears.

He heard me silently to the end; then convulsively grasping my hands, was completely overcome by his feelings, and we wept together.

"Ah, Geoffrey, my cousin, my more than brother and friend," he said at last, "how gladly would I confer upon you, if it would increase your comfort and happiness, the envied wealth which has been the fruitful cause of such revolting crimes!

"Ah, mother!" continued he, looking up to the calm heavens, and raising his hands in a sort of ecstasy, "dear, sainted, angel mother, whom as a child I recognized and loved, it is only on your account that I rejoice—yes, with joy unspeakable, that I am indeed your son—that the boy you so loved and fondly cherished, was the child you sought in heaven, and wept on earth as lost. And that fine, generous, noble-hearted old man—how proud shall I feel to call him father, and recall all his acts of kindness to me when a nameless orphan boy. And Margaretta, my gentle sister, my best and earliest friend. Forgive me, dear Geoffrey, if thoughts like these render me happy in spite of myself. I only wish that you could participate in the fullness of my joy."

"I will—I do!" I exclaimed, ashamed of my past regrets. "The evil spirit of envy, George, cast a dark shadow over the sunshine of my heart. This will soon yield to better feelings. You know me to be a faulty creature of old, and must pity and excuse my weakness."

Unconsciously we had strolled to the top of a wild, heathery common, which overlooked the marshy meadows below, and was covered with dwarf oaks and elder-bushes.

Though close upon day-break, the moon was still bright, and I thought I discerned something which resembled the sharp outline of a human figure, suspended from the lower branch of a gnarled and leafless tree, the long hair and garments fluttering loosely in the wind. With silent horror I pointed it out to my companion. We both ran forward and soon reached the spot. Here, between us and the full, broad light of the moon, hung the skeleton-like figure of Dinah North, her hideous countenance rendered doubly so by the nature of her death!

Her long grey hair streamed back from her narrow contracted brow; her eyes wide open and staring, caught a gleam from the moon that heightened the malignant expression which had made them terrible to the beholder while in life.

We neither spoke, but looked at each other with eyes full of horror.

George sprang up the tree and cut down the body, which fell at my feet with a dull, heavy sound.

"She has but anticipated her fate, Geoffrey. Surely the hand of God is here."

"Miserable woman!" said I, as I turned with a shudder from the livid corpse—"is this the end of all your ambitious hopes? Your life a tissue of revolting crimes—your end despair!"

We hurried back to the cottage to give the alarm, and found Robert Moncton awake and in his senses, though evidently sinking fast. "Dinah North dead!" he said, "and by her own voluntary act. This is retributive justice. She has been my evil genius on earth, and has gone before me to our appointed place. Geoffrey Moncton, I have a few words to say to you before I follow on her track.

"I have injured you during my life. I have, however, done you justice now. I have made you my heir; the sole inheritor of the large fortune I have bartered my soul to realize."

"But, uncle, you have a son."

His face grew dark as night.

"None that I acknowledge as such. And mark me, Geoffrey," and he compressed his lips firmly and grasped my hand tightly as he spoke: "I have left you this property on one condition, that you never bequeath or share one copper of it with that rascal Theophilus Moncton, for in such case it will benefit neither party, but will revert to your cousin, Margaretta Moncton. Do you hear?" and he shook me vehemently.

"And what will become of Theophilus?"

He laughed bitterly. "He will yet meet with his deserts," he exclaimed. "What I have done may seem harsh to you, Geoffrey, but it is strictly just. My reasons for so doing may puzzle the world and astonish professional men, but it is a secret which never will be known until I meet the human monster, who calls himself my son, at the eternal bar. And may the curse of the great Judge of all flesh, and my curse, cleave to him for ever!"

I shrank back from him with feelings of disgust and horror, which I took no pains to conceal; but it was unnoticed by him. The hand relaxed its rigid grasp, the large icy eyes lost the glittering brilliancy which had marked them through life, the jaw fell, and the soul of Robert Moncton passed forth from those open portals to its drear and dread account.

"He is dead," said the lawyer.

I drew a long sigh.

"How did he come to his death, young gentleman?"

"He was shot from behind the hedge, as he rode through the pit at the end of the long plantation. He said, when we first found him, that he knew the person who shot him."

"He admitted the same thing to me, but would not mention the name of the assassin. I have my own suspicions."

I had mine, but I did not wish to hint at the probability of a fact that Robert Moncton had purposely, I have no doubt, left unrevealed. The cause of his death, and the hand which perpetrated the deed have never been discovered, but will remain open to conjecture as long as those live who feel the least interest in the subject. It was supposed, that important information could be obtained from his son, which might throw some light upon the mystery, but he had disappeared, and no trace of his whereabouts, could be discovered.

We were detained for several days at the village whilst the coroner's inquest sat on the bodies, and we had made a statement before the proper authorities of all we knew about this mysterious affair.

Before three days were at an end, the public journals were filled with accounts of the awful tragedy which had occurred at the village of ——, in Yorkshire; and the great talents and moral worth of the murdered lawyer were spoken of in terms of the highest praise, which certainly astonished his relations, and would have astonished himself. The only stain on his character, it was stated, was the extraordinary manner in which he had disinherited his only son, in order to place a *poor relation* who had been brought up in his house, in his shoes. It was evident to all, the part this domestic sneak must have acted in the dreadful tragedy to ensure the property to himself.

Hints of a darker nature were thrown out, which deeply wounded my sensitive pride, and which drew a reply from Mr. Blake, who stated, that Mr. Moncton told him that the murderer was well known to him, but he never would reveal to any one who or what he was; that he left young Geoffrey Moncton and George at the inn, and they did not come up until after he was shot. That the assassin did not attempt to conceal himself, but exchanged words with him and met him face to face.

I had just taken up my pen to add my testimony to that of the worthy Mr. Blake, when the door of the room suddenly opened, and Sir Alexander and his lovely daughter, banished all other objects from my brain.

What an overflowing of eyes and hearts succeeded that unexpected meeting. How I envied George the hearty embrace with which the fine old man received his newly recovered son. The tearful joy which beamed in the dark eloquent eyes of his delighted sister as she flung herself with unrestrained freedom into the arms of that long-cherished friend, and now beloved brother.

My welcome was not wanting either: Sir Alexander received me as another son, and my own, my lovely Madge as something dearer to her than even a brother.

CHAPTER XIV.

THE DOUBLE BRIDAL.

The first excitement of our meeting over, I was painfully struck with the great alteration that the absence of a few weeks had made in the face of Margaret.

Her eyes, always beautiful, gleamed with an unnatural brilliancy; and her pure, pale complexion, at times was flushed with a hectic glow, which, contrasting with the dazzling white teeth and jet-black hair, gave a fearful beauty to her charming face.

I took her hand in mine. It burned with fever.

"Dear Margaret, are you ill?"

She raised her eyes to mine, swimming in tears.

"Not ill, Geoffrey; only a little weak."

"No wonder, when you are in such a state of emaciation. You ought not to have let the death of Alice bring you so low as this."

"Your absence and long silence, dear Geoffrey, have had more to do with my poor health than the death of my unfortunate friend."

"How so, dearest?"

"Torturing anxiety, sleepless nights, and days of weeping, would produce this change in stronger frames than mine: But that is all past. I am quite well and happy now, and Margaret will soon be herself again."

This was accompanied by such a sad, moonlight smile, that it only served to increase my fears. I inquired earnestly if her father had consulted a medical man.

"Oh, yes—a dozen, at least."

"And what opinion did they give?"

"They told the plain truth—said that my illness was produced by mental excitement—that change of air and scene would soon bring me round."

I felt that I looked grave and sad. She put her arm round my shoulder, and whispered in my ear:

"You are mine, Geoffrey, and I shall soon get well in the society of those I love; so banish that gloomy frown, and try to participate in the general joy. I have procured an excellent flute for you, as a little present. You shall play, and I will sing, and Kate Lee (of whom I am no longer jealous) and George shall dance, and papa shall smoke his cigar beneath our favourite old tree and enjoy the fun; and we shall all be so happy."

Thus did my poor, fading, white rose strive to divert my thoughts into a brighter channel; and hope, ever attendant upon the young, cheated me into the belief that all would yet be well.

Instead of returning to Moncton Park, George proposed our accompanying him to Elm Grove. Sir Alexander thought the change would be beneficial to Margaretta, and we joyfully accepted his proposal. I exchanged my horse with Sir Alexander, and took his place by the side of Madge in the open carriage. The good Baronet rode with his son, who had a thousand revelations of his past life to communicate to his delighted father.

Madge and I were not without our histories and confessions; and long before we entered the avenue that led to Elm Grove, the dear girl had promised to become my wife, when returning health should remove the last barrier to our union.

Our reception at Elm Grove was such as might have been expected from its amiable possessors.

Accounts of Robert Moncton's and Dinah North's death had travelled there before us, and formed for the first few days the theme of general discussion. My kind friend, Mrs. Hepburn, warmly congratulated me on my accession of fortune, and Dan Simpson was almost beside himself with joy. Though I could no longer regard myself as Sir Alexander's successor, I found myself not a whit inferior in wealth and importance.

Sir Alexander received my proposal for his daughter with unfeigned satisfaction. He wrung my hand with hearty good-will. "Two sons, my dear Geoffrey. God has given me two sons in return for depriving me of one of them for so many years. Faith, my dear boy, I hardly know which is dearest of you to the old man. Madge, however, has found out which of the twain she loves best. I shall resign the Hall to George and his pretty bride, and will come and live with my dear girl and my adopted son—hey Madge! will you give the old man an easy place by your fireside?"

Margaret threw herself into his extended arms, parted the white wavy locks from his high forehead, and devoutly kissed it.

Thus did we suffer hope to weave bright garlands for the future, without reflecting how soon the freshest flowers of life are withered and scattered in the dust.

Cheered by the society and sympathy of her new friends, with a devoted lover ever at her side, Margaretta regained much of her former health and cheerfulness.

Hand in hand we roamed among the Derby hills, and visited every romantic spot in the neighbourhood, not forgetting the old parsonage where my mother was born, the spot where my good old grandfather was buried, the little inn over which Mrs. Archer presided, who was infinitely delighted with seeing me again, and hearing me introduce her lovely boy to Margaretta's especial notice.

Kate Lee did the honours of the house with the most bewitching grace, and she and Margaretta formed the most lively attachment to each other.

"Is she not beautiful, Geoffrey?" said Margaretta, as we sat together on the lawn beneath the shade of a large ash; and she watched her friend as she bounded past us down the grassy slope, to join Sir Alexander and his son in their evening walk.

"Yes, very beautiful, Madge."

"Don't you envy George the possession of such a charming wife?"

"I love George and admire his Kate, but I would not exchange my little fairy," and I pressed her fondly to my heart, "for his stately queen."

"Ah, flatterer! how can I believe you, who would prefer the pale, drooping snow-drop to the perfumed, glowing rose?"

"Let George keep his rose, the peerless among many sweets, but give me the pure solitary gem of early spring, which cheers with its modest grace the parting frowns of envious winter."

I pressed her small white hand with fervour to my lips and heart. The meek head of the gentle girl sunk drooping on my bosom. The long black lashes that veiled her matchless eyes were heavy with bright tears.

"Why do you weep, sweet Madge?"

"I am too happy. These are tears of joy: they relieve the fulness of my heart. After suffering so much bitter grief it is a luxury to weep in the arms of the beloved."

How often have I recalled those words when weeping in madness on her grave, and found no joy in grief—no peace in my distracted heart.

The harvest had been gathered in, and the ripe autumnal fruits hung heavily on the loaded trees when we returned to Moncton Park. The first of October had been named for the celebration of our double nuptials, and all was bustle and activity at the Hall, in making the necessary preparations for the important event. Margaretta appeared to take as much interest in the matrimonial arrangements as her lively friend, Kate.

Not a ribbon was selected or a dress purchased, but George and I were called to give our opinion of its beauty or becomingness; whilst the good old Baronet's whole time and attention were directed to the improvements and decorations which he had planned in the interior of the Hall. Thus all went merry as a marriage bell until the second week in September, which was ushered in by heavy gales and frequent showers.

Often, when returning from our accustomed rides and walks, Margaret would draw her shawl tightly round her, and clinging closely to my arm, would complain that she was *cold—very cold.*

One day in particular, when the deceitful beauty of the morning had induced us to extend our ride a few miles farther than usual, we all got drenched by a sudden shower of rain. The next morning my dear girl complained of a pain in her chest, sudden chills and weariness of mind and body. These symptoms were succeeded by a short, hacking cough, and sudden flushings of the face, which greatly alarmed us all. Medical advice was instantly called in, but Margaret's malady daily increased and her strength rapidly declined.

I dared not whisper to myself the fears which oppressed my heart, and was almost afraid of asking Dr. Wilson the nature of her complaint.

To my utter grief and despair he informed me that his patient was beyond human aid—that a few weeks, at the farthest, would terminate the existence of the gentlest and purest of human beings.

"It would be cruel to deceive you, Mr. Moncton," said he, as he announced the startling truth—for the dreadful communication had quite unmanned me. "Let this comfort you in your affliction, that I have anticipated this for years; that our dear patient has carried about her the seeds of this fatal malady from infancy; that it is better that she should thus fall in the budding season of youth, than leave hereafter a family of children to bewail their irreparable loss. I sorrow for her father and you, Mr. Geoffrey, more than for her. Death has few terrors to a sincere Christian, and such from childhood Margaret Moncton has been. A friend to the friendless, a sister of mercy to the poor and destitute."

Oh, reader! if you have ever known what it is to see your fondest hopes annihilated at the very moment of their apparent fulfilment, you can form some idea of my mental anguish whilst watching the decay of that delicate flower.

Margaret was now fully aware of her danger, a most uncommon circumstance in the victims of that insidious disease, on whom Death advances so softly that he always comes suddenly at last. She prepared herself to meet the mighty conqueror with a cheerful submission to the will of God, which surprised us all.

One thing she earnestly entreated, that the marriage of Catherine and George might not be postponed on account of her illness.

"I not only wish to witness their happiness before I go hence, but to share in it," she said to us, a few days before the one which had been appointed for the ceremony, as we were all sitting round the sofa on which she was reclining.

"And you, dearest Geoffrey, must give me a lawful claim to the tender care I receive from you. Though I can only be your wife in name, I shall die happy in hearing you address me by that coveted appellation."

I could in reply only press her wasted form in my arms and bathe her hands and face with my tears. How earnestly had I wished to call her mine, though I lacked the courage to make the proposal so dear to my peace.

Oh, what a melancholy day was that to us all. Margaret's sweet face alone wore a serene smile, as, supported by her father, she stood beside me at the altar.

How beautiful she looked in her white bridal dress. What a mockery was the ceremony to my tortured heart, whilst fancy, busy with my grief, converted those flowing garments into a snowy shroud.

One little week after that melancholy event I again bent before that altar, to partake of the last tokens of a Saviour's dying love; but I knelt alone. The grave had closed over my bright, my beautiful, my virgin bride, and my soul had vowed an eternal divorce from the vanities and lusts of earth.

Years have fled on in their silent and undeviating course. I am now an old, grey-headed man.

Sir Alexander Moncton has long been gathered to his fathers, and the old

Hall is filled by a race of healthy, noble-looking young people, the children of Sir George Moncton and Catherine Lee. I, too, have a Geoffrey and a Margaret, the children of my adoption; for a large family Sir George willingly spared me these.

For years I have resided at the Lodge, formerly the residence of Dinah North, which I have converted into a pretty dwelling, surrounded by shrubberies and flower-gardens. I love to linger near the scenes where the happiest and saddest moments of my life were passed.

Behold me now, a cheerful and contented old man, surrounded by dear young faces, who lavish upon Uncle Geoffrey the redundant affections of warm and guileless hearts.

My wealth is the means of making many happy, of obviating the sorrows of the sorrowful, and smoothing with necessary comforts the couch of pain. When I first lost my beloved Margaret, I mourned as one without hope; but it pleased God to hallow and bless my afflictions, and by their instrumentality gently to lead me to a knowledge of the truth—that simple and holy truth, which has set me free from the chains of sin and the fear of death.

In what a different light I view all these trials now. How sincerely I can bless the munificent hand which wounds but to heal—punishes but to reform; who has poured upon the darkness of my soul the light of life, and exchanged the love of earth, which bound me grovelling in the dust, for the love of Christ; sorrow for the loss of one dear companion and friend, into compassion for the sorrows and sufferings of the whole human race.

A few words more, gentle reader, and we part for ever. These relate to the fate of Theophilus Moncton, and fully illustrate the awful text—"There is no peace," saith my God, "for the wicked;" and again, "The wicked have no hope in their death."

From the hour that Robert Moncton fell by the hand of the unknown midnight assassin, Theophilus Moncton was never seen or heard of again for upwards of twenty years, until his name was forgotten, and I, like the rest of the world, believed that he was dead, or had become a voluntary exile in a foreign land.

One day, while crossing the Strand, just below Somerset House, my charity was solicited by the dirty, ragged sweeper of the street.

The voice, though long unheard, was only too familiar to my ear, and looking earnestly at the suppliant, with mingled sensation of pity and horror, I recognized my long-lost cousin Theophilus Moncton.

He, too, recognized me, and dropping the tattered remains of his hat at my feet, muttered half aloud:

"Do not betray me, Geoffrey; I am a lost and miserable man. My punishment is already greater than flesh and blood can well bear."

"What assistance can I render you?" I asked, in a faltering voice, as I dropped my purse into his hat, for the sight of him recalled many painful recollections.

"You have rendered me the best in your power;" and flinging away his broom, he disappeared down a dirty, narrow alley, leaving me in a state of doubt and anxiety concerning him.

Wishing to convert this sinner from the error of his ways, and to elucidate if possible the mystery which involved his father's death, I repaired to the same place for several days in the hope of meeting with him again, but without success.

A week elapsed, and I found another son of want supplying his place at the crossing of the street. Dropping a shilling into his extended hand, I asked him what had become of the poor fellow that used to sweep there.

"Saving your honour's presence," returned the mendicant, in a broad Irish accent, "he was a big blackguard, and so he was, not over-honest neither, and always drunk. T'other day, some foolish body who had more money nor wit, took a fancy to his ugly, unwholesome phiz, and gave him a purseful of gould —or mayhap he stole it—an' he never quits the grip of the brandy-bottle till he dies. They carried the body to the poor-house and that's all I knows of the chap. 'Tis a lucky thing, yer honor, that the scamp has neither wife nor child."

I thought so, too, as with a heavy sigh I took my way to the inn, murmuring to myself as I walked along:

"And such is the end of the wicked."

THE END.

CPSIA information can be obtained
at www.ICGtesting.com
Printed in the USA
LVHW110100010920
664725LV00011B/811